Deadly Encounter . . .

Umberto Sanchez's back straightened with alarm when he heard something slice through the air, followed by a sound similar to a machete chopping a melon. He turned to see his partner, still on horseback behind him. Blood bubbled from the stump of the man's neck, dying his shirt bright red. The headless corpse toppled from its saddle and Umberto saw the tall figure with the long sword standing among the boulders behind the victim.

The bandido swung his revolver at the samurai, cocking the hammer as he aimed. Tanaka Tom held the *katana* in his right hand and snapped his left down from his ear, releasing a *shuriken*. Umberto saw the blur of the star-shaped object streaking toward him. He tried to dodge the projectile and failed to fully cock his gun—self-preservation taking priority over killing the samurai. The *shuriken* slammed into his forehead, the sharp tines biting into bone to pierce his brain. Umberto Sanchez died in the twinkling of an eye, and fell from his horse, the unfired Colt still in his hand.

Tanaka Tom Fletcher shook the blood from his `katana` and climbed down from the boulders. He pried the throwing star from the dead bandido's forehead and replaced it in his *obi*. The samurai climbed unto the back of Umberto's horse, satisfied that his karma had looked upon him with favor. . . .

The Six-Gun Samurai Series:

FROM THE LAND OF THE SHOGUN

#6

SIX-GUN
SAMURAI

BUSHIDO LAWMAN

Patrick Lee

PINNACLE BOOKS   NEW YORK

SIX-GUN SAMURAI #6: BUSHIDO LAWMAN

Copyright © 1982 by W. L. Fieldhouse

An original Pinnacle Books edition, published for the first time anywhere.

First printing, February 1982

ISBN: 0-523-41418-8

Cover illustration by Bruce Minney

Printed in the United States of America

PINNACLE BOOKS, INC.
1430 Broadway
New York, New York 10018

To Erik Bock, my instructor in *kenjutsu*. Many thanks and best wishes for your future.

Patrick Lee

PROLOGUE

The legend of the Six-gun Samurai officially began in the small town of Washout, Nevada in 1873 when a tall, slender stranger—dressed in an incredible manner and armed with two swords—entered an obscure saloon and decapitated a hardened gunman named Frank Tollar. However, the seeds of the samurai's past had been sewn two decades earlier when twelve-year-old Tommy Fletcher served as a midshipman to Commodore Perry on his first voyage to the mysterious Asian country Westerners called Japan.

A remarkable series of circumstances plunged young Tommy into his destiny. *Ninja* espionage agents assaulted the American mission, forcing the boy sailor to flee for his life. All but naked and stranded in a land where the culture, language, and customs were totally alien to his own, Tommy wandered the streets of Edo, living on what scraps of food he could find and fighting off other urchin youths to retain each meager prize. Then he literally ran into Tanaka Nobunara, a young samurai knight-warrior who was in the service of the *shogun*.

Impressed with Tommy's spirit and intelligence, Tan-

1

aka adopted the boy. Raised as a samurai, Tanaka Tom Fletcher became a great warrior and acquired the rank of *daimyo*—warlord fourth class—the first American to attain such a high position of Japanese nobility. Tom might have remained in *Dai Nippon* for the rest of his life, an honored and successful member of the imperial elite, if fate had not decreed otherwise.

Isaac Tomlinson, a close friend of the Fletcher family in Georgia and now a general in the United States Army, contacted the American embassy in Japan to relay grim news to Tanaka Tom. The Fletcher family had been massacred by the Bummers under command of General Sherman. Led by the ambitious and ruthless Colonel Edward Hollister, they slaughtered Tom's parents, sister, and younger brother and sacked the Fletcher plantation.

Tom's older brothers had both died on the battlefield during the War Between the States, thus he alone remained to avenge the murder of his blood relatives as required by *bushido*, the code of the samurai.

Tanaka Tom Fletcher, the product of a culture little known to Americans and trained in the martial arts of a Japanese knight-warrior, returned to the United States. His first effort to locate Edward Hollister promised to solve his quest rapidly. This encounter cost the lives of many of Hollister's men, but the evil colonel managed to escape the samurai's lightning sword.

Tom's next venture took him to Arizona Territory, where one of Hollister's ex-officers, Captain Bradford Cone, attempted to cause an Indian war in order to claim gold on Apache land to serve as capital for the colonel's insidious plans to conquer the American West.

Next, the Six-gun Samurai clashed with Jeffery Nash, a corrupt politician in San Francisco, who was trying to seize control of the city to further Hollister's evil scheme. Again the colonel eluded him as Tom fought Nash and the deadly Blue Dragon Tong. His fourth mission in New Caanaland, Colorado, pitted him against the sinister community, a perverted religious society led by their false prophet, the Reverend Bradly Ashton. Most recently, Tanaka Tom had completed his battle against Sergeant Major Kitchner and his attempt to gain control of an enormous silver deposit in Nevada.

A telegram from General Tomlinson directed the samurai to the next leg of his vengeful journey. Eddie Mears, formerly a corporal under Hollister's command, had been arrested for cattle rustling in the small New Mexican town of Marzo Viento. Although rustling was too small an operation to interest the ambitious colonel, Mears might be able to supply Tom with information about Hollister's whereabouts and plans for the future.

Confident in his abilities with Western firearms, as well as his assortment of samurai weapons and skills, Tanaka Tom continued his *bushido*-bound mission. *Karma*—his personal fate—would guide him in his task. If the Six-gun Samurai failed in his duty to avenge his slain ancestors, he would be required by honor to commit *seppuku*—to disembowel himself—to cleanse his soul. This prospect did not frighten Tanaka Tom Fletcher. It would also be his *karma*.

One

The hot afternoon sun seemed to challenge the tall rider as he allowed his Morgan stallion to assume its own leisurely pace. The arid prairies of the New Mexico Territory were inhospitable to man and beast alike. Tanaka Tom Fletcher would not demand more from his horse and the gray pack mule that followed his mount, than they could safely bear in such a climate. Although he had to get to Marzo Viento before the circuit judge could pass sentence on Eddie Mears, a dead animal wouldn't help him accomplish anything.

An inch above six feet tall, Tom's long slender frame was accustomed to travel on horseback. He had grown to favor the large Western saddle to the Japanese riding gear he'd been trained to use as a samurai in *bajutsu* (the art of horsemanship).

His high cheekbones and hawkish nose revealed the Cherokee blood of his otherwise Caucasian heritage. An almond-shaped cast to his dark eyes and his straight black hair also hinted of his Indian ancestry. The Levi's trousers and gunbelt, with its well-oiled .45 Colt revolver holstered on his left hip, were customary attire in the American West, but his other garments and weapons seemed as out of place in this environment as a teacup in a saloon.

Tom wore a short *kimono* jacket, bound together by a yellow silk *obi* (sash) around his narrow waist. His samurai boots were made of soft leather and did not feature spurs. Thrust through the sash were two swords—the long *katana* and the short-bladed *hotachi*—the traditional weapons of the samurai.

Tanaka Tom Fletcher's mind relaxed as he rode. The past is gone and useful only for the memories and knowledge that can be applied to the present. The future is *karma* and will unfold as it must, regardless of desires, hopes, or schemes. There is only the present. At that moment, the Six-gun Samurai's *present* was a barren range of sand, sagebrush, and rock formations.

The terrain offered a primitive beauty, which Tom appreciated in the practical manner of a Japanese knight-warrior who enjoyed watching the sun splash color on the dawn sky and wrote *haiku* poems when mood and circumstances moved him. Gazing at the majestic red and yellow stone walls, the verses of a poem formed within his head.

Silent giants, sleep not nor wake
Sentinels of time,
Who outlive man.

Tom mentally chided himself for allowing his thoughts to concentrate on any single feature of his surroundings. His mind needed to remain relaxed and tranquil, a mild state of oblivion acquired through deep meditation. The prairie might contain unseen perils. Thoughts and speculation would not reveal these hazards, but might instead serve to misguide his attention from where danger lurked. He would observe all things equally and keep his consciousness blank. His reflexes and skills would rescue his body from any harm that

5

might befall it. If not, karma would come to claim his soul.

Yet, even with his disciplined mind, Tom found it difficult to repel memories and apprehension. Perhaps this was because the New Mexican range reminded him of the Imperial Valley in California. In that blistering desert, he had encountered three escaped convicts from Yuma Prison. The incident nearly cost him his life. Such a deadly chance-meeting might occur again. Unconsciously, his left hand moved to the walnut grips of his Colt as he approached the rock formations he had admired scant seconds before. If someone intended to ambush him, this would be the obvious place from which to launch the attack—perhaps *too* obvious.

Tom glanced casually around the stone walls but failed to notice the short, wiry figure that rose among some boulders to his right. Suddenly, he saw the interloper, a thin-faced man, boldly swinging something attached to a cord overhead. The Samurai's revolver cleared leather, but the ambusher had already released his device. The weighted cord whistled harshly and sliced through the air toward the samurai. Tanaka Tom leaned to the side, attempting to dodge the unfamiliar projectile, but it proved to be deceptive. A lead filled ball attached to a cord struck him between his left temple and ear. Starlike explosions erupted painfully inside his head. A soft black blanket consumed him and Tanaka Tom Fletcher toppled from his saddle.

Carlos Alverez whooped in triumph when he saw the rider collapse silently to the ground. He climbed from the boulders and dragged an ivory handled .44 Remington revolver from his belt holster. Four other figures emerged from their positions on the rock walls and hurried to join Carlos, who scrambled down the stony formation to inspect his victim.

"Ah, *mis compañeros*," he laughed. "You are my witnesses. When next you hear my brother's friends talk of his prowess with the *bolas*, you tell them that *El Halcón* is a man of great skill, but Carlos Alverez is even greater!"

"*Sí*," Manuel Gonzales nodded. An unwashed bandido with a set of prominent buck teeth that jutted from his black matted beard without revealing his lips, Gonzales had learned the wisdom of agreeing with the man in charge—even if that man was a silly *cachorro*, obsessed with proving his *machismo*. "You threw the *bolas* with the eye of an eagle and the sureness of a bullet. Your brother will be proud when we tell him how . . ."

"¡ *Maldecir mi hermano*!" Carlos snarled. "I do not care what he thinks. I will tell him how easily I killed this *gringo* pig without firing a shot—and you will tell him as well—but Fidel will only shrug and mutter that he has done as much many times before." The seventeen-year-old bandit smiled thinly. "Yet inside, he will be jealous of what I've done today."

Manuel nodded vigorously. The others followed his example and chanted, "Sí, sí," as they bobbed their heads. Carlos Alverez was an immature little fool, but he was a dangerous little fool and the brother of El Halcón.

"This gringo is quite a prize, Carlos," Raul Rodriguez, a fat, greasy bandido remarked, licking his thick lips with expectation. "Look at how full his saddle bags are and that mulo is heavily packed as well. ¡*Madre de Dios*! Luck has smiled on us this day!"

"I do not think this man is *all gringo*," Pedro Morales commented. The skinny outlaw turned Tom over with the toe of his boot and examined him with a brooding expression on his gaunt face. "He may have been part *mexicano* or maybe *indio*. Look at his features."

"Whatever he was part of," Carlos growled, stepping

closer to kick Tanaka Tom's ribs with contempt, "he was all *cabrón*."

"Sí," Manuel added with a chuckle. "And now he is *un cabrón muy muerte!*"

"Let's see what the Anglo pig has brought us for our trouble," the teen-age bandit leader instructed. "Search his animals."

Carlos frisked the samurai's still body as the others examined the pack on the mule and the saddle bags. They cheered gleefully when they discovered sacks of gold nuggets and bundles of greenback dollars. Opening one of the parfleche containers strapped to the mule, Pedro grunted with satisfaction as he extracted a long bow and a heavy wooden quiver equipped with two dozen arrows.

"It is as I suspected," he announced. "The gringo was part indio as well."

"I never saw an Indian with a bow like that," Manuel said. "It is longer than any I know of. And—who ever heard of a Yaqui or an Apache who carried his arrows in a fancy box like that?"

"Maybe he was from some tribe we never heard of." Pedro shrugged, now bored with the mystery. He tossed the bow and arrows aside. "I don't know why he bothered to pack these things when he has a fine repeating rifle in that saddle boot."

"That Winchester belongs to me," Carlos told them. "One of you can have the *bastardo*'s short gun and—" The youngster's sentence ceased abruptly when he tugged the sharkskin wrapped handle of Tom's katana. *"Cristo,"* he whispered, his eyes widening at the sight of the long, polished blade that slid from the lacquered scabbard in the samurai's *obi*.

"It is a sword," Raul said, too amazed to feel stupid about such an obvious statement. "I have never seen such a sword!"

"Magnifico," Carlos mused, examing the three-foot-

long blade of the finest steel he had ever seen. The slanted point puzzled him for a moment, but he decided it would stab as well as any rapier or saber. The sword was heavier than the cavalry saber his older brother once carried as an officer in the Bolivian Army. He wondered if it would cut as well as Fidel's sword. Carlos tested the edge with his thumb.

"*¡Que la chigada!*" he cried, jerking the digit away from the *katana*. Blood trickled from the hairline thin, but surprisingly deep, cut. "I barely touched it. *Cristo,* this *espada* is sharper than a razor!"

"What sort of man is this?" Pedro wondered aloud. "He carried guns and arrows and a sword . . ."

"No!" Carlos exclaimed in amazement as he pulled the *ho-tachi* from Tom's sash. "He carried *two* swords! One a smaller version of the other!"

"*¿Dos espadas?*" Manuel raised an eyebrow. "Why?"

"Maybe he has a derringer as well," Raul suggested. "Or some more money."

Carlos jerked off Tom's *obi*. His *tanto* knife and five star-shaped metal objects fell to the dust. "He had this *cuchillo* and some sort of amulets," the bandit remarked. "Probably some kind of *indio* good-luck charms."

"May as well leave them," Raul grinned. "They must not work very well."

"What will you do with the swords, Carlos?" Manuel inquired.

"The long *espada* is mine," the youthful bandido replied. "I will give the short one to my brother. It will always remind Fidel of what I've done this day." He laughed bitterly. "And that *my* sword is greater than his."

"That is a fine knife, Carlos," Raul remarked, staring at the *tanto* lying on the ground beside the motionless Tanaka Tom.

"Take it," the teen-age bandit shrugged. The swords had pleased him enough to feel a sliver of generosity.

Raul bent to gather up the *tanto*. The cloth of Tom's kimono stirred slightly by his diaphram. The bandit snatched up the knife with an alarmed gasp and reached for the old Griswald & Gunnison .36 caliber cap and ball revolver on his hip.

"I think he's still alive!" the fat bandido declared, his voice revealing a surprising amount of fear for an unconscious opponent.

"Don't be ridiculous," Carlos scoffed. "No one could survive a blow from my *bolas*."

"Perhaps we should put a bullet in his head just to be certain," Manuel suggested.

"There is no need to waste ammunition on a dead man!" Carlos shouted angrily. "Do you doubt my ability?"

"Of course not," Manuel assured him.

"Sí," Raul agreed. "I just have been mistaken. Perhaps the wind moved his jacket."

"Afraid of the wind, Raul?" Carlos smirked. "I hope you all stop acting like old women by the time we reach Marzo Viento."

"Marzo Viento?" Pedro inquired, a startled expression on his thin face.

"Sí," Carlos nodded. "If Raul is frightened by a little breeze, he may be terrified by a town called 'March Wind.' "

"Why are we going there?" Manuel asked. "It is only a small *aldehuela*, hardly worth our time."

"It has a bank," Carlos replied. "Even a small bank has money. Before we return to my brother's camp, I intend to have enough to show him that El Halcón is not as great a bandido as he thinks himself to be."

The others were less than enthusiastic about the proposal. They had just robbed a rich traveler and acquired a great deal of valuables in the process. Surely, it was not wise to tempt their good fortune in such a rash manner. However, Carlos was in charge and they had to follow his orders. They began to repack the mule when Pedro decided to see what the other parfleche contained.

"¡Sancta Madre!" he whispered, extracting a wooden mask from the bag. Artfully crafted and boldly painted, the expression of a warrior's fury was frozen on its face. "Have we robbed a man or a demon from hell? Can such a creature be killed so easily?"

"Stop talking like a superstitious peón!" Carlos snapped. "Leave the mask if it bothers you so, but we keep the parfleche. We will examine it more closely later."

Tossing the samurai fright mask to the ground beside the kyujutsu bow and arrows, Pedro quickly closed the bag on the mule's back. He glanced at Tanaka Tom with dread. They shouldn't simply ride off with this man—if he was a man—just lying on the ground. They should first fire a silver bullet into his heart or cut off his head and stuff garlic or salt into his mouth. Old wives' tales, perhaps, but Pedro couldn't cast off the sensation that they had encountered something they didn't understand—something that would cost them dearly in the future.

Tanaka Tom Fletcher awoke with a groan. A throbbing pain above the mastoid bone behind his ear forced his eyes shut. The right side of his face, exposed to the sun, felt hot and sore. Slowly, he moved his head, grinding warm sand into his left cheek. His neck appeared to be intact. Other than the dull agony inside his head, he seemed to be uninjured. Resisting the urge to simply keep his eyes closed and drift into a natural sleep, Tom flexed his fingers—his hands and arms were not damaged.

Suddenly, a loud, hostile rattle filled the samurai's ears. Although the sound assured him his hearing had not been impaired, it was hardly comforting. Something hissed sharply like water hitting a hot rock. Slowly opening his eyes, Tanaka Tom Fletcher found himself face to face with a seven-foot-long diamondback rattlesnake.

Two

The serpent, coiled like a satanic rope, cautiously watched the Six-gun Samurai, its cold reptilian eyes unblinking and the sensitive forked tongue flicking in and out with apprehension. The snake had crawled to the rock formation in search of shade from the relentless sun. At first, it mistook Tom for a stationary object, but drawing closer, realized the man was a warm-blooded creature.

Hungry, the rattler appraised its intended victim, its delicate tongue sensing that the man was too large to swallow and thus unsuitable prey. Then the samurai moved. The reptile shook its tail in warning and prepared to strike.

Tanaka Tom felt his heartbeat quicken as he breathed shallowly to avoid disturbing the snake. His left hand crept with glacial slowness to his hip. Frustration and anger billowed inside his aching head when his fingers touched the empty holster.

The snake hissed violently, its rattle shaking harder as it sensed the man's hostility. Tom forced his emotions from his consciousness and carefully slid his hand to his waist. The *obi* sash was missing. Tom's eyes widened with a new realization that overwhelmed his concern about the deadly serpent less than three feet away. His swords were gone.

"Eeya," he hissed, more vehemently than the rattler. "Someone has stolen my honor!"

Alarmed, the serpent's heart-shaped head hurled forward, its jaws opening to bare long curved fangs. Tom's adrenaline-charged body rolled aside. The snake's deadly mouth brushed the lapel of the kimono as its strike fell only inches off its target. His samurai-trained reflexes as fast as the snake's, Tom jerked his torso aside and swung his left arm. The side of his hand slammed into the serpent's neck, pinning its head to the ground.

Holding the poisonous skull stationary, Tom's other hand seized the reptile's angrily rattling tail. Rising to his knees, the samurai breathed deeply into his *hara,* an inch below his navel. Then he released the snake's neck while he pivoted on one knee, swiftly grabbing its tail with both hands.

Before the rattler could alter its striking position, Tom swung it overhead like a *kusarigama* sickle and chain weapon. With a *kiai* shout, he hurled the snake's head into the rock wall. Twice more the samurai swung the serpent, dashing its skull into the unyielding stone, before tossing it aside.

The snake twisted in the sand as its body refused to acknowledge death. The spade-shaped head had been crushed, its brains splattered from a deep split between its sightless eyes. At last, the desperate rattle ceased and the dead reptile lay still.

Tanaka Tom rose stiffly to his feet. His encounter with the serpent proved his body and reflexes had not been impaired by the blow to his head. Yet, his health remained a secondary concern. His *daisho,* the traditional long and short swords of a Japanese knight-warrior, had been stolen. A samurai's sword is more

14

than his life. One dies to be reborn, but the *katana* is the soul of the warrior. Without it, he is not whole. Even the Japanese ideograph for "man" is the symbol of a sword with an added brush stroke to indicate possession. Until he regained his *katana* and *ho-tachi*, Tom would not be a man. He would not be a samurai. The fact his other belongings had also been taken only disturbed him mildly compared to the loss of them.

Tom dusted off his *obi* before binding it around his waist. He grunted with restrained satisfaction when he discovered the five *shurikens* had been discarded by the thieves. Westerners seldom recognized the five-pointed stars to be weapons. Tucking the *shurikens* into his sash, the samurai moved to his *kyujutsu* bow and arrows.

Tanaka Tom felt a contradictory and somewhat illogical anger that his archery equipment had been left by the robbers. To ignore his fine *take* bow and *naka-zashi* war arrows was almost an insult. However, he realized few Americans—except Indians—appreciated such weapons. Made of a special hard bamboo, the rattan-bound bow and its bone and horn tipped missiles were an integral part of the samurai's arsenal. The leather and lacquered wood *ebira* quiver contained the traditional twenty-four arrows, varied in length and design to suit different needs and situations.

Attaching the *ebira* to his hip, he gripped the bow and notched the bowstring in the *tsurugami* manner. Then he noticed the samurai fright mask staring up at him near his feet. So, these highwaymen would treat his armor with disrespect as well! Tanaka Tom vowed to find the men who dared to dishonor him. He would see them die or take his own life to compensate for his shame. He wondered if the loss of his swords and his failure to avenge himself on Edward Hollister might be too great a disgrace for even *seppuku* to erase. He would not concern himself with such thoughts. His karma would decide his fate and he could only do as circumstances required.

Although his samurai training had included the mastery of numerous weapons and abilities, tracking had not been one of them. Fortunately, Carlos Alverez and his bandidos had not tried to cover their trail, so even an inexperienced tracker such as Tanaka Tom would have little difficulty following their hoofprints in the sand.

Despite the merciless heat and the seemingly endless headache, Tom continued to walk after the thieves. His samurai riding boots were not designed for travel by foot, but Tom accepted the blisters on his soles as a mere discomfort. Perhaps his karma decreed that he must suffer certain agonies as payment for the loss of his swords. The samurai would endure any hardship if he could reclaim his sacred weapons.

His adopted father, Tanaka Nobunara, had given him the swords when he was seventeen and he had been officially ordained as a samurai by the shogun himself. The *katana* and *ho-tachi* had been in the Tanaka family for more than two hundred years. The ancestors of Tom's adopted father would judge him most harshly if he did not retrieve these noble weapons.

As the sun began to descend into the Western horizon, the temperature fell in the curious dramatic manner of desert regions. Tanaka Tom continued to follow the tracks until the darkness was too dense to allow him to see the hoofprints. Reluctantly, he lowered himself to the ground, accepting the setback as yet another part of his karma. The bitter cold combined with hunger to deepen his misery. Tom hoped it would prove to be Fate's punishment for allowing his swords to fall into unworthy hands, and an indication that he would soon pay his debt to the cosmic forces of destiny and find his prized weapons.

16

Dealing with hunger was a simple task for a samurai. He merely concentrated his *hara* to cause his stomach to feel full. The cold was more difficult. Through the power of *ki*—the inner or spiritual force of Man—he could increase his body heat to its maximum and warm himself for an indefinite period of time. However, this would consume a great deal of energy, and he could not afford to confront his enemies in a weakened state.

Assuming the half-lotus position for *zazen* meditation, Tom folded his hands on his lap, the right thumb resting on the left. The wind swept against his exposed face and hands, the chill cutting through the thin fabric of his clothing. The samurai did not attempt to ward off the icy sensation. Blending with it, he allowed his body temperature to drop like a cold-blooded creature—like the serpent he'd killed that day. The clammy texture of his skin slowly lost its unpleasantness as Tom became one with the cold.

The chill could not harm him for he was part of it and it was part of him. His flesh remained still as his mind and spirit—his *ki*—joined the wind. Tanaka Tom and the wind were everywhere, brushing the sands of the New Mexico prairie and reaching out to the stars of the night sky above. They moved without ceasing, effortlessly and beyond exhaustion—with the peace of eternal strength and the immortality of the elements.

At dawn, the Six-gun Samurai continued to follow his quarry. The tracks remained remarkably legible to Tom's untrained eye. He smiled. It was a good omen, evidence that his karma and his honor would reunite if he did not deny his duty. Armed with his *kyujutsu* bow and the *ebira* quiver on his hip, Tom walked in the direction of his horse-bound opponents.

As the earth slowly heated in the morning sun,

Tom's body released itself from the night's icy grip. His flesh welcomed the warm, gentle massage, but the samurai kept his mind free of this simple pleasure. A warrior must always remain alert, expecting nothing and prepared for anything.

Two miles from where he'd spent the night, Tanaka Tom encountered the remnants of a camp. The bandidos had fenced in their horses with a rope corral tied to some ocotillo cactus and a mesquite tree. Flattened ground revealed where their sleeping blankets had been. Tom crouched by the ashes of a crude campfire. Burned tumbleweeds crumbled at his touch, but some greasewood, charred beneath, was still warm. Horse droppings were only beginning to become dry and hard.

Still tracking the bandits, he approached a now dusty arroyo, flanked on either side by hulking ocher boulders. At first a sound like distant waves striking the shore puzzled him. The noise grew closer and Tom knew what it was: A dozen or more galloping hooves. Quickly, he moved to the cover of the boulders, extracting his first *nakazashi* arrow as the riders appeared from the east of the gully.

Four men on horseback galloped into view. They wore standard Western garb, Levi's trousers, denim workshirts, and practical Stetson headgear. Leading the group was a large, barrel-chested man astride a handsome Appaloosa stallion. His clothing appeared to be less trail-worn than the other riders, and a stern, grim expression was etched into his proud, wedge-shaped face. Two of his companions also seemed to regard their task as an unpleasant, but somehow necessary chore. The fourth and last man, however, smiled wickedly, revealing large tobacco-stained teeth amid the whisker stubbles on his narrow face.

Tom frowned, lowering his arrow. These men may or may not be the highwaymen that ambushed him, but Tanaka Tom didn't see his horse or mule or any of his equipment. Although he'd only glimpsed the man who'd thrown the slinglike weapon at him, the samurai didn't think any of these riders was his assailant. Perhaps they'd seen the thieves. Judging from their expressions, Tom decided it would not be wise to question them, so he remained hidden and watched.

As the riders galloped farther into the arroyo, he noticed that three men in the rear had ropes tied to their saddlehorns. They were dragging something fiercely across the rough, sunbaked ground. Dust settled around the objects at the end of the lariats. It was a man, his tattered clothing stained with dirt and blood. From the unnatural position of his arms and legs, Tom guessed all four of the man's limbs had been broken. The leader of the horsemen jerked back the reins of his Appaloosa and brought it to a halt while he held up a hand to signal his men to do likewise.

"Is he still alive?" the stern-faced figure asked in a deep commanding voice—the voice of a man accustomed to being obeyed.

"Hard to say, Mr. Wilkins," the thin rider with the sadistic smile replied, gazing down at the dragged man with malicious delight. "He's plenty busted up, that's for sure."

Wilkins grunted with satisfaction. Pulling the reins to the right, he forced his mount around and rode to the motionless, broken body. His steely gray eyes observed their victim without sympathy.

"Want us t'drag th'bastard some more, boss?" the toothy sadist inquired hopefully.

"No need, Clay," Wilkins replied flatly. "He's paid for rustlin' cattle from the Big W spread." He calmly drew a .45 caliber Colt from a hip holster and shot the prone figure twice—one bullet smashing under the left shoulder blade into the victim's heart and the other shattering the base of his skull.

19

"If'n we bury this jasper, you want a headstone for him?" Clay asked lightly. "How th'hell do ya spell 'Mears' anyway? Sounds sort'a like 'smears' don't it? We sure smeared him all over th'territory today!"

"Naw—Mears is like a lookin' glass, ain't it?" another rider remarked. " 'M-I-R-O-R-S.' "

"He sure don't look like much now," Clay giggled.

"His kind don't deserve no funeral," Wilkins declared gruffly. "Leave him for the buzzards and the coyotes. There's more work waitin' for you back at the ranch."

Mears, Tom thought tensely. The man he'd come to the New Mexico Territory to find. Somehow Wilkins and his men managed to get Eddie Mears out of the Marzo Viento jail. Frustration and disappointment churned within the samurai while he watched the cowboys remove their ropes from the mangled corpse before climbing back into their saddles. Tanaka Tom waited until the four riders galloped out of view before he emerged from the rocks and moved to the still body of Eddie Mears.

The Six-gun Samurai didn't bother to check for a pulse in the mutilated lump of torn flesh and tattered cloth. Even if the brutal dragging hadn't killed him, two well-placed forty-five rounds insured no life remained in Mears's body. Tom turned the corpse over with his boot, his toes feeling the splintered ribs under Mears's skin. Little remained of the outlaw's face. Nearly all the flesh had been scraped away from his cheeks and mouth and his nose had been sheared off, leaving only a bloody cavity. Both eyes remained intact, wide-open and filled with pain and terror.

The ghastly sight did not disturb Tom. He had discovered long ago that man's cruelty to his fellow man is universal and subject to no restraints due to nationality or race. The samurai searched the dead man's pockets,

20

hoping to find some scrap of information about Hollister. There was nothing. Anything Eddie Mears may have been able to tell Tom about his archenemy had been terminated with his life. Now Tanaka Tom Fletcher had only one reason to remain in the New Mexico Territory—to recover his swords.

Wearily, the samurai located the bandidos' trail and continued to track the robbers. After several minutes of following the hoofprints, he decided the four men he'd watched kill Mears could not be the thieves. The tracks were too fresh for the outlaws to have circled around and headed back to the arroyo. Tom was pleased to discover still moist horse droppings on the trail, which would dry up rapidly in the noon-day heat. He must be closing the distance between himself and his quarry. The knowlege restored his hopes and added fuel to his determination.

He walked less than a mile farther before he saw the town. Consisting of only fourteen buildings, including private homes, it was a small community. Four structures were made of brick or adobe and the rest were constructed of wood. Only the local saloon reached three stories high. A sign at the town limits informed him that he was about to enter Marzo Viento.

Tom snorted sourly. His original destination no longer contained the man he'd traveled so far to question. Yet, the bandidos' tracks extended to the town. A strange sensation crept through Tom from his *hara* to his chest. For some reason, known only to the Powers of Destiny, this place was part of his karma. A series of events had directed and guided him to Marzo Viento. He could no more avoid entering this town than he could avoid his own death when the time for his passing arrived. Tanaka Tom Fletcher walked into Marzo Viento, confident he would either regain his honor or lose his life.

Three

If awards had been given to sleepy border towns that had warranted little note in the history books, Marzo Viento would have ranked at least third place—until that day. Destiny, or perhaps karma, had selected it for a bloody chapter in the saga of the American West and the legend of the Six-gun Samurai.

The streets of Marzo Viento were generally uncrowded. Clem Porter, an emaciated old-timer who spent every cent he earned on rotgut whisky and cheap tequila at the Sommer Place Saloon, was the first to notice the stranger. Porter squinted and strained his alcohol-corroded eyes, trying to appraise the stranger. At first he thought Tanaka Tom might be a little tipsy himself, since the samurai walked unsteadily on weary legs and blistered feet.

A glimpse of Tom's face quickly dispelled Porter's notion that the newcomer might be a fellow drunkard. The man's sleek head and proud features were determined and alert. Although Porter could not see Tom's eyes because of the shadow from the cone-shaped hat of woven rice-reeds, he suspected the stranger's orbs would be as unflinching and all-seeing as a young eagle's. He noted the man's ramrod straight posture and his deceptively lean frame, guessing that this peculiar looking person was more muscular than he appeared.

Accustomed to appraising a man by his appearance instead of his belongings or items he happened to be carrying, Porter noticed the hawkish shape of Tanaka Tom's nose and the high set of his cheekbones before he saw the *take* bow in the stranger's hand. An Indian, he decided. Maybe only part Injun, but half-breeds tended to be even tighter with a dollar than their full-blooded counterparts, Porter thought unhappily. Funny-looking bow and quiver he carried, in fact everything about the newcomer seemed strange. The old-timer had never seen a Chinaman, but he'd heard they wore odd headgear like this man's, but he'd also heard they were little fellers too.

Porter couldn't recall ever seeing an Indian, or anyone else, carrying arrows in a fancy wooden boxlike quiver on the hip before. At least the man didn't carry a gun. Porter didn't trust Indians—even part-Indians— with firearms. Maybe this feller *was* a Chinaman, a big one or a half-breed yellow-boy. Porter didn't like the idea of any nonwhite or anyone with mixed blood, carrying guns. Maybe this newcomer, whoever and whatever he might be, was a hunter who'd got lost and headed for Marzo Viento to get directions. A Chinese half-breed might just be more generous than one with Indian blood in his veins.

Porter licked his lips. Shoveling horse dung all day had added to his incurable thirst for liquor. Hell, he thought, he'd finished cleaning up half of the livery stable. That ought to be enough to earn half of the twenty-five cents Jacob Fritter, the local balcksmith who owned the stables, paid him for the job. If he could convince the stranger to give him a dime or even a nickel, he'd have enough to buy a couple of beers or maybe a shot of redeye. Better yet, he could take the newcomer's donation, run over to the saloon, have a quick drink and hurry back to the stable and finish his original task. A lot of effort, but it'd be worth it for some mind-easing alcohol.

Porter briefly wondered what his mind needed to be eased of. He vaguely remembered a farmhouse he'd owned . . . twenty, maybe thirty years before. He had a wife then . . . Jenny or Julie, he couldn't recall the name for certain although her face returned clearly to his mind's eye. She had been young and pretty with a bright expressive face framed by long chestnut hair. She was pregnant that day the Yaquis or the Apaches, or whatever brand of red devils they were, had attacked their farm.

Porter had returned home to find the house little more than a charred pile of lumber, smoke still curling from its gutted, burned remains. He found Janet—*that* was her name—nailed to a giant X constructed from two fence posts by the raiders.

They'd pinned her to the frame and raped her repeatedly, until her naked vagina resembled a butchered rabbit. Then they sliced off her breasts like a pair of fleshy melons. Her teeth had been knocked out and her nose cut away, creating the appearance of an obscene jack-o-lantern. Janet's tormentors had gouged out her eyes and squished them like a pair of blood-filled grapes. Worse, they'd carved open her bloated belly and pulled the unborn fetus from its mother.

Porter remembered gazing down from the mutilated remnants of his wife to stare at the small, dead embryo at his feet. Covered with blood, the partially formed baby remained attached to its umbilical cord. Tiny but distinctly human fingers clutched at its narrow chest. The disproportionately large head seemed bowed forward in pain, its little mouth open in a cry that would never be heard. His child had died before it ever truly lived. Boy or girl? Porter never knew.

His entire world destroyed in one afternoon, he'd gone berserk. Porter gathered up his old Sharps rifle and mounted his piebald gelding, determined to find the men responsible for the vicious atrocity that robbed him of his family, his home, and a large portion of his sanity. Clem Porter must have ridden a thousand miles in his quest for vengeance, but he never found a single man who'd been involved in that grotesque incident.

One day, he quit searching and sold his Sharps and his horse and the well-worn saddle. In frustration and sorrow, he drank himself into a stupor. The liquor softened his anguish and helped him to forget the mangled, ragged face of his murdered wife and the pitiful little corpse the monsters that walked like men had torn from its mother's womb. Liquor accomplished what revenge had not. He could close his eyes and dream of Janet and honestly believe she would be waiting for him when he returned to a home that no longer existed.

Clem Porter never went home, because when he awoke, he knew there was nothing there but the rotting corpses of the only two persons he'd loved and could not bring himself to bury. Eventually, Janet became a creature of mist within his mind and he dreamt only of the next bottle. Revenge and love dissolved with the years of excess drinking. Only his desire for oblivion remained.

The town drunk's hands trembled, nearly dropping his shovel as memories long buried arose and brought his all-but-forgotten grief to the forefront of his mind. He had to drive the thoughts back into the deep, cobweb-covered caverns from whence they came. They were painful. God, they hurt like red-hot spikes inside his head. Tears brimmed over the lower lids of Porter's eyes as he staggered over to the stranger.

"Hey, Mister?" he began, his voice as shaky as his fingers. "I could surely use a coin or two if you can spare it."

Tanaka Tom Fletcher glared at the drunkard, his face a mask of anger and resentment. He had come to this town in search of his swords. His honor and the name of the Tanaka ancestory were in jeopardy, yet this filth-encrusted beggar dared to bother him when such important matters were at hand. The samurai resisted an urge to cuff the impudent vagabond and curse him for his annoyance. He turned to verbally order the old man from his sight and warn him never to approach him again.

Then he saw the pain in Clem Porter's eyes and he recalled another beggar, a twelve-year-old beggar who'd wandered the streets of Edo. A frightened little boy, far from home and loved ones he would never see again. Alone in a strange country on the other side of the world.

"I am sorry," he said gently. "I have no money. Perhaps later."

"Sure, Mister," Porter replied, his voice crushed by disappointment. He bowed his head and turned from the samurai. For the first time in more years than he could be certain, Clem Porter felt shame for what he had become. It was yet another burden for his agonized soul to cope with, another ghost to be slain by more alcohol.

Tom continued to walk through the nearly deserted streets of Marzo Viento. A scrawny yellow-brown hound appeared from the alley between the Sommer Place Saloon and the general store. It barked an angry warning at the stranger. Tom ignored it and moved forward. The dog splayed its legs and growled, lips curling back to reveal sharp teeth. The samurai glanced at the animal with contempt and walked on.

Realizing the man was not afraid and sensing he had no reason to be concerned with his territoral invasion the hound tucked its tail between its hind legs and shuffled in a rapid sideways gait away from the stranger. It howled occasionally as if trying to regain some dignity from the confrontation.

"Didn't figure nothin' could spook that old cur, young feller," a gruff voice declared.

Tom turned to face the speaker. A plump, middle-aged man sat on the plankwalk beneath the legend that announced his occupation to anyone able to read English or Spanish.

"That's right, feller," the man grinned as he doffed his battered black stovepipe hat. "I'm Oscar Brill, the local *director de funeraria*. Undertaker sure sounds better in Mexican, don't it?"

"I am Tanaka Tom Fletcher," the samurai replied with a polite nod.

Brill smiled. "That's a powerful lot of name. Hate to have to put it on a headstone. Wouldn't hardly leave no room for the dates."

"I have no need of headstones," Tom assured him.

"We all die, feller," the mortician declared with a satisfied nod, as if everyone would one day be his personal customer and this somehow protected him from a similar fate. "What do folks call you that ain't got half the day to do it?"

"You don't seem very busy," the samurai commented dryly.

"I got a feelin' business is about to improve a bit," Brill mused, lighting a cigar stump as shabby-looking as his old hat.

"What do you mean?" Tom demanded, sensing the undertaker's words were not idle conversation.

Brill blew a smoke ring into the air. The lack of breeze allowed it to drift skyward before it slowly dissolved into a string of gray mist. "What do folks call you again?"

"Take whatever part of my name you wish and address me as such," the samurai replied with annoyance.

"Tanaka is a different sort of handle for a feller," the

27

mortician said with a pleased nod. "Ain't never met no Tanaka before."

"Most would not be as tolerant as I," Tom said stiffly.

"That so?" Brill smiled smugly. "You look to be part Injun. Even if you didn't have them bow and arrows, I'd guess there was a little red-nigger crawlin' around in your blood."

Tom's eyes hardened, but he didn't fail to notice the butt of a Remington revolver worn in a cross-draw position on the undertaker's belt. A mocking smile turned the samurai's face into a sinister mask. "Are you trying to make some business for yourself, Mister Brill?"

"Just tryin' to avoid becoming part of it," the mortician replied. "My partner couldn't embalm a dead sparrow so's it'd last a week," Brill stroked his fleshy chin thoughtfully. "Tanaka an Injun name of some sort?"

"Japanese," Tom answered, his voice a challenge for the undertaker to make light of it.

"Do tell," Brill grinned. "Well, if'n you die in Marzo Viento you'll have to settle for your name in English or Spanish lingo on the stone. All I know about Japanese is it looks like some sort of pictures Old Clem over there might draw."

"All written language is derived from pictorgraphic symbols," the samurai told him coldly. "And Clem's company has been favorable to your own."

"Easy, Tanaka," Brill said around his stogie. "You tell me what you want to know and I'll see if I can oblige, but unlike Clem I won't ask you to buy me a drink afterwards."

"Why do you say your *trade* might improve soon?"

"Because you and them other fellers that arrived here today all got the stink of death about you," the mortician answered.

"These other men," the samurai's voice became urgent. "What are they like? Where are they now?"

"Five Mexican fellers," Brill replied. "Mexicans I don't mind for the most part. Hard workin' people, and Spanish is a right pretty language," he frowned. "But 'these fellers have trouble written all over them. I figure they're bandidos for sure. They was carrying guns hung low on their hips and bandoliers criss-crossin' their chests. Real bad *hombres*. Rode their horses like they was born in the saddle. Just like a bunch o' hill bandits."

"Where are they?" Tom repeated. "Did any of them have a pair of swords? One long and the other roughly half its length?"

"Didn't notice no swords," the undertaker shrugged, tossing the tiny plug of burning tobacco into the street. "They headed down the street somewheres. Probably gone to the Sommer Place Saloon. You'll see their horses tied to the hitchin' rail, I suppose. One of them fellers rode a real fine white Arabian and most of the others had mustangs and cross-breeds. Oh, yeah," Brill smiled. "Also led a big Morgan and a gray pack mule just loaded with possibles. Sound familiar?"

Tom nodded grimly. "You have less honor than a jackal, scavenger, but I thank you for your information."

"Helpin' folks is my job, Tanaka," Brill chuckled.

The Six-gun Samurai dismissed the undertaker's verbal cat-and-mouse game. He had more important matters to consider than Brill's disrespectful nature, which he suspected the mortician directed toward everyone in general and strangers in particular. Tom walked toward the Sommer Place Saloon, his mind too troubled to notice the beauty of the vivid pale blue sky or the mesquite trees that seemed to reach from the ground to greet the yellow sun. He didn't fail to notice the six horses and a pack mule tied to the hitching rail in front of the town bank.

Tom drew a *nakazashi* war arrow from his *ebira*

29

when the first shot exploded from within the bank. Manuel Gonzales and Hector Vargas, a broad-faced bandido with long, unwashed black hair bound by an Indian headband to keep it from distorting his vision, emerged from the building, pistols and bulging canvas bags in their hands. Shouts of alarm and fear mingled with the second gunshot. The samurai leaped to the cover of a water trough and fell to one knee.

A young red-haired man appeared from the sheriff's office, sunlight flashing on the copper deputy badge pinned on his denim shirt and the metal frame of a .45 Army Colt in his fist. Another man, older, slower-moving and thicker at the waist than the deputy, followed him outside with a short-barreled shotgun in his steady hands. Tom notched the arrow to the bowstring as the younger lawman and the bandits exchanged fire.

Deputy Jeremy Pike pulled the trigger too quickly, failing to aim as he rushed forward. The lawman's bullet whined fiercely and ricocheted off the brick wall behind Hector. Manuel's shot was equally unsuccessful. A poor marksman and armed with a seldom-cleaned .36 caliber Hopkins & Allen revolver, the bandit's round struck the wooden support of a porch roof five feet from its intended victim.

Sheriff Hal Newton fired one charge from his double-barreled Greener. He realized the range to be too great to use the scattergun effectively, but hoped the blast would force the bank robbers to hold their fire long enough to allow the lawmen to get closer. The tactic worked. Manuel and Hector bolted from the plankwalk and jumped to the cover of their horses.

Tanaka Tom Fletcher drew the bowstring back slowly until the feathered tip of the *nakazashi* touched his cheek. He breathed slowly and steadily while he aimed with the skill acquired in twenty years of *kyujutsu* archery. Tom released the bowstring.

The war arrow whistled angrily as it cut through the air. Manuel Gonzales's mouth opened in an effort to scream. His eyes bulged in his dirty face and he staggered backward. The feathered end of the arrow jutted from the right side of the bandit's neck, the bulk of the shaft and the "turnip's head" point protruded from the other side—dyed red with Manuel's blood. The bandido crumpled to the ground and died.

Hector Vargas realized the new threat and turned his Navy Colt toward the bowman. He was too late. Rapidly, but accurately, Tanaka Tom readied another *nakazashi* and launched it at the shaken bandit. The arrow slammed into Hector's barrel chest, the sharpened-horn point piercing his heart before bursting through his back below the left shoulder blade.

Carlos Alverez and Pedro Morales burst from the bank, six-guns spitting lead. Deputy Pike, as surprised by the archer's assistance as the bandidos, had just begun to take advantage of the distraction Tom's role in the carnage had created. Pike charged closer to the bank robbers, exposing himself to their fire. A .44 slug plowed into his chest near the star-shaped badge. Another bullet struck the point of his chin and shattered his jawbone, but the deputy didn't feel it. Jeremy Pike was already dead.

Pedro continued to fire at the remaining lawman and forced the sheriff to retreat into an alley between the jailhouse and the local barber shop. Carlos Alverez, half crazy with anger and fear, charged Tom's position, his ivory handled Remington blazing in his fist.

Due to the samurai's kneeling position and the fact he'd chosen to wear the *ebira* quiver on his hip instead of on his back, canted to his shoulder, Tom didn't have time to draw, notch, and fire another arrow. Carlos's hastily aimed shot burned air near Tom's left ear. The bullet shattered a window of the saloon behind the sam-

31

urai. Tanaka Tom's left hand dove to his *obi* while the bandit cocked the hammer of his Remington.

A star-shaped object flashed in the sunlight as it whirled from the samurai's fingers like a metal meteor. Carlos screamed when the sharp tines of the *shuriken* bit into his face, piercing soft flesh to lodge firmly in his cheekbone. The young bandido stumbled, jerked the trigger of his pistol to blast a round into the sky, and toppled to the ground with an agonized moan.

Tom reached for another arrow, but the sound of a revolver hammer cocking into place arrested his movement. He stared into the muzzle of the old Whitney Colt in Pedro Morales's hand. The bandit had dashed across the street when he saw Carlos fall—and now he had the Six-gun Samurai at his mercy.

"You!" Pedro exclaimed, his eyes expanding with recognition. "I knew we should have made certain you were dead," the pistol shook in his unsteady hand. "*¡Mueras, brujo!*"

The shot boomed like the eruption of a cannon. Tom stared in amazement as nine double-0 buckshot pellets tore into the clothing and flesh of Pedros Morales, ripping his shoulder to shreds and obliterating the right side of his face. The force of the blast hurtled the bandit into an awkward cartwheel, the Whitney Colt falling from his lifeless hand.

Pedro Morales crashed through the batwings of the Sommer Place Saloon. His corpse sprawled onto the sawdust covered floor to the startled horror of the patrons within—none of whom had any desire to get involved in the gun battle outside.

Sheriff Hal Newton jogged toward Tom, the Greener in his grasp held across his chest. Smoke still curled up from one barrel. The samurai recalled another shotgun blast that had saved his life in San Francisco—fired by another officer of the law.

"You hurt, feller?" the sheriff asked breathlessly.

32

Five and a half feet tall, Newton carried an additional girth of middle-age and inactivity around his waist. His pale blue eyes and the expression on his angular face revealed his genuine concern for the stranger's well being.

"Yes," Tom replied. "Thanks to you."

"Thank *you*, Mister," Newton said. "Appears you did most of my job for me."

Sudden movement in front of the bank drew their attention. Raul Rodriguez had cowered within the building while his fellow bandits exchanged shots with Tom and the lawmen. Terrified, the fat outlaw retained only one desire: to escape.

He hauled himself onto the back of his Morgan-mustang cross-breed with amazing speed for a man of such bulk. The hoofs of his mount nearly trampled the still-groaning figure of Carlos Alverez. Newton cursed under his breath and shifted the scattergun to one hand and drew his sidearm. The samurai notched an arrow to the string of his bow, but the panic-stricken Raul had already galloped out of accurate range. The sheriff also held his fire.

"Damnation," he muttered. "Instead of jawin' away, I should have made sure none of those bastards was left."

Tanaka Tom Fletcher didn't hear the sheriff's words. He hurried to the animals still tied to the hitching rail, desperation blending with expectation as he searched their saddles. Newton watched with confused astonishment.

"What the hell you lookin' for, feller?" he asked.

Tom sighed with relief when he found the ornate handle of his *ho-tachi* jutting from a saddle bag. The *katana* had been bound to the horn of Carlos's saddle with a length of rawhide. The samurai anxiously tore his weapons from the bandido's leather. Newton shook his head.

"What are those things?" the baffled lawman inquired.

"My soul," Tom explained, nearly weeping as the burden of his loss lifted from his shoulders. "My honor is once more intact."

"If you say so, feller," Newton agreed with a shrug.

Four

After the fighting ended, the people of Marzo Viento slowly ventured from the surrounding buildings. They murmured in muted despair at the sight of the corpse-riddled street. Several pointed at the dead bodies and shook their heads grimly. A few, mostly Mexicans dressed in ill-fitting work clothes, sombreros, and sandals, crossed themselves and whispered prayers of mercy for the departed souls and for divine protection from a similar fate.

Oscar Brill didn't appear the least bit upset. The undertaker marched into the street with a cheerful hum escaping around the fresh cigar in his mouth. He pushed the stovepipe hat back from his forehead with a thumb and examined Carlos Alverez. The bandit lay spread-eagle on his back, the *shuriken* still lodged in his bloodied cheek.

"Hell, this feller ain't dead," Brill muttered with disappointment.

"No," the Six-gun Samurai remarked. "He will not die from his wound. I usually dip the points of my *shurikens* in poison, but that one has not been treated since last it met human flesh."

"Poison, eh?" the mortician grinned. "I like your style, Tanaka."

Brill walked to the bodies of Manuel and Hector. "You surely did a better job with these two," he mused. "Sure you're a Japman and not an Injun? These arrow shots would do a Cheyenne dog soldier proud."

"Jeremy's dead," Sheriff Newton announced, his drooping gray-streaked mustache accenting his frown.

"I'm right sorry 'bout that," the undertaker said, but his voice revealed no remorse. "I'll give the Pike widder my condolences along with my bill."

Newton glared fiercely at Brill. The mortician merely smiled and knelt by the corpse of Manuel Gonzales. He plunged a hand into the dead man's pockets and extracted several coins and greenbacks.

"Before you remove any of their belongs, understand that they robbed me and much of what they have is rightfully my property," Tom warned softly.

"Sort'a figured that," Brill shrugged.

The samurai curtly nodded.

"That where you got them things stickin' in your sash, huh? Off'n them dead bandits?" the mortician inquired. "Didn't notice 'em before."

"What all did these fellers take from you, Mister?" Newton asked the stranger.

"My name is Tanaka Tom Fletcher and they stole my horse, pack mule and supplies—including several thousand dollars in gold and currency."

"Not to mention those swords," Newton remarked.

Tom was mildly surprised by the sheriff's observation since most Westerners failed to recognize his *katana* and *ho-tachi* as weapons. "That is correct," he said. "The Winchester in that saddle boot is mine also," he pointed at the rifle sheathed on the back of his Morgan. "As well as a forty-five caliber Colt revolver."

"Ain't it convenient that they took all this gold you

36

claim they stole," Brill commented cynically, fearing his profit would slip away.

"If they have that much gold I reckon they took it from Mister Fletcher or he wouldn't have known about it," the sheriff snapped.

"Sure wouldn't figure they'd be interested in a little ol' bank like what we got here if'n they got that much loot," Jacob Fritter stated. The six-foot-two blacksmith scratched his bearded chin thoughtfully, the bulky muscles of his triceps and biceps straining the fabric of his longjohn shirt.

"Bandidos is greedy jaspers," Fred Utley, the owner of the local general store mused. Short and portly, Utley wore pin-striped trousers with a matching vest and a white shirt, stained yellow at the collar, cuffs, and armpits. "Guess they never have enough."

"At least they didn't rob anyone's hard-earned savings here in Marzo Viento," a tall gaunt figure declared as he emerged from the bank. He wore an Eastern suit, tailored to his long slender build, with a gold watch chain extending between the pockets of his vest. His thin gray-haired head turned toward Tom. "My name is Arnold Dell, young man. I'm the owner of the bank and the mayor of Marzo Viento. I saw how you bravely fought these villains, armed only with a primitive bow and arrow. I commend your courage, sir. And I thank you for rescuing my bank from these thieves."

"Somethin' our sheriff and his deputy couldn't seem to manage all by themselves," Bart Finely, the sour-faced bartender from the Sommer Place Saloon commented.

"Ease up, Bart," a feminine voice urged sharply. "Since you didn't go into the street to take a chance on catchin' a bullet, don't criticize them that did."

"Hold on, Amanda," Joel Stewart, the stocky owner of a tannery and leather shop, began. Although Stewart

37

made saddles and holsters, the bulk of his profits in Marzo Viento depended on his ability to repair shoes and boots.

"*You* hold on," the woman snapped. Thirty-one-years-old, she'd retained a lovely hour-glass figure and her dark red hair was as untouched by gray as her smooth oval face remained clear of wrinkles. "You were all mighty good at holdin' back when the shooting started!"

"We ain't gunfighters, Miss Sommer," Burl Davidson whined. As emaciated as Clem Porter, the Marzo Viento barber gazed sheepishly through the lenses of his wire-rimmed glasses. "That's why we pay our lawmen to handle that sort'a thing." He bobbed his head in confirmation of his own statement.

"Nobody paid this feller," Amanda Sommer cast an admiring glance at Tanaka Tom Fletcher, pleased to notice the interest expressed in his dark almond-shaped eyes. "But this stranger didn't run for cover."

"He don't know the town good enough," Finely muttered.

"Old Tanaka here had his own business to settle with them Mexican owlhoots," Brill remarked. "Speakin' of business, ain't another feller lying in your saloon in need of my services?"

"Go help yourself, you two-legged buzzard," Amanda answered with disgust.

"All vultures have two legs, my dear," the mortician remarked. "The lucky ones have wings and are able to fly from dreary places like this town." he smiled. "But don't worry. My feathers ain't ruffled."

"Appears to me you could use some restin' up," Newton told Tom. "You oughtta get yourself a room for the night."

"Thank you, Sheriff," the samurai replied. "I would also like a bath."

38

"Bathin' can wait," Jacob Fritter declared. "First, I'm gonna buy this feller a drink!"

Several other voices announced their intentions to do likewise. Clem Porter staggered into the crowd, hoping some of their newfound generosity would fall on him. Amanda Sommer raised her hands for silence and decleared that the first round would be on the house. The cheering men practically swept Tom up as they charged into the saloon. Oscar Brill dragged the body of Pedro Morales through the batwings a moment before the mob entered the building.

Sheriff Newton pulled the *shuriken* from Carlos's face. The young bandit groaned loudly as a fresh wave of pain summoned him back to consciousness. The mortician approached the lawman.

"Tanaka sure uses some queer weapons, don't he?" Brill commented.

"Yeah," Newton agreed. "And he sure uses them good."

Carlos rose to his hands and knees. He touched his damaged cheek and sobbed like a child.

"On your feet, Mister," Newton ordered, aiming the bandido's own Remington revolver at him. "Jailhouse ain't far and you can rest up in a cell as long as you like."

"At least until the circuit judge shows up," Brill added.

"My men," Carlos whined. "What happened to my men?"

"Everybody's dead 'cept for you and a fat boy who run out on you," Newton replied. "Now, get up."

"The gringo," the bandit's eyes hardened in their moist sockets. "The one with the bow. Did I get him?"

"He got you, kid," the undertaker chuckled. "That's how come you ain't so pretty no more."

A cold smile appeared on Carlos's blood-stained

face. "It doesn't matter. You will all be dead for your actions this day."

"You can tell me all about it in the jailhouse," Newton said.

A pinch-faced figure dressed in a black suit with a clerical collar and a bearded Mexican in similiar garb, shuffled into the street while Carlos slowly climbed to his feet.

"Sheriff, Father Santos and I wish to have a word with you," the taller clergyman announced.

"Not now, Reverend Baker," Newton replied.

"As the spiritual guardians of the people of this community, we cannot stand by and allow this drunken orgy to occur!" Baker declared.

"Sheriff," Santos began, his voice thick, suggesting he consumed wine more often than Holy Communion was served in his church. "The dead men are Mexicans and thus, we must assume they are Catholic . . . or were. It is only proper they receive a proper funeral with religious services."

"Those three fellers are probably in hell by now," Brill snorted. "Besides, funerals is my business. I don't tell you two how to baptize babies."

"Evil souls are in greater need of our prayers than the rest of us, *Señor* Brill," the priest replied. "But since none of their families are here to contribute to the collection plate—and such things as candles and Communion wafers cost money . . ."

"Sheriff, I've told you before about that woman and her den of iniquity," the reverend snapped. "She's leading those men down the road of damnation with her alcohol and . . . whatever else they serve in that cursed place. If you can't force her to close down and leave the community, at least do something to prevent the drunken disorder that will occur tonight!"

"Excuse me, gentlemen," Arnold Dell said. "I'm going to that 'den of iniquity' and buy Mister Fletcher a

40

drink. By the way, Mister Brill. The bank robbers killed my bank teller, Jeff Colby. See to him, will you?"

"My pleasure," the undertaker grinned. He turned to Newton. "Hard to tell which of us is the busier today, ain't it?"

"Disgraceful conduct," the Reverend Baker sighed.

"Amen, Preacher," Brill chuckled.

Sheriff Newton escorted Carlos Alverez to the jail, ignoring the bandit's claim that they'd soon beg him to take the money from their bank.

"Wonder how long that Tanaka feller is going to be in town," the mortician mused, blowing a smoke ring thoughtfully.

"The man is an instrument of violent destruction." Baker shook his head woefully.

"What is this man's religion?" Santos asked. "Is he Catholic?"

"He's probably whatever Japmen are," Brill shrugged.

"A heathen as well as a killer!" the reverend exclaimed. "I pray he does not remain in Marzo Viento past sunup."

"I sort of hope he stays awhile," the undertaker commented. "Feller sure is good for business."

Amanda Sommer and Tanaka Tom Fletcher unsteadily mounted the stairwell, their arms encircling each other's shoulders. She giggled as her foot slipped from a step and the samurai's strong grasp saved her from a punishing tumble down the stairs. A small rational part of Tom's brain chided him for drinking too much.

He hadn't been intoxicated since he attended the feast of Lord Fumio, a *daimyo* friend of his adopted father, Tanaka Nobunara. He'd consumed great sums of rice wine and enjoyed a variety of delicacies. His

41

hashi chopsticks plunged into plates of *sashimi* raw fish, *nori* seaweed and spicy *tori no mizutaki* chicken and vegetables. With *gohan* boiled rice and *senbei* crackers, the meal was enormous and exhilarating compared to the generally restrictive and bland diet of a samurai.

The excessive *sake* warmed Tom's stomach and lulled him into a restful slumber. He awoke to find himself in the sleeping quarters of Mikko-*san,* Fumio-*sama's* most favored concubine. The pleasure of discovering the beautiful white-skinned Mikko lying beside him on the *tatami* mat was erased by the shocking knowledge that he had abused the hospitality of the *daimyo* who had honored him with the invitation to the feast. This disgrace was an insult to Fumio-*san* and to the family of Tanaka. His dishonor had to be dissolved or his spirit would be cursed to a lowly rebirth and the Tanaka name would be blighted and shamed.

Although a samurai, the eighteen-year-old Tanaka Tomi Ichimara had never before been faced with a situation that demanded the act of *seppuku*. He had seen men disembowel themselves for their failure on the battlefield or upon command by their ruling *daimyos*. His American roots shunned suicide, yet his culture required it. Could he actually insert the blade of his *hotachi* into his intestines and pull the razor edge across his belly? He imagined his guts spilling onto the *tatami* floor, pink serpents bathed in blood—his blood.

He sat on his knees in position and drew the short sword from its scabbard. Tomi's hands were steady as he reversed the grip and pointed the blade at his midsection. His heart raced fearfully, his mind recoiling from the terrible pain and death he was about to inflict upon himself.

"Eeya, Tanaka-san!" Mikko cried. *"Eeya!"*

Tomi barely heard her plea. Beads of sweat popped from his forehead as he lowered the slanted tip of the *ho-tachi* to his kimono. He forced his breath into his *hara* to control his terror. His death was necessary. He owed it to the noble ancestors of the Tanaka family—ancestors of the great samurai class—to take his life as tradition demanded. Mikko padded from the room and cried for help, but Tomi did not hear her. His entire being remained concentrated on the ritual of *seppuku*.

The sword point pressed firmly. It pierced cloth and touched his skin, barely breaking the surface. For one panic-stricken moment, the young samurai prepared to pull the blade away. Then a strange tranquility replaced his terror. Tomi was no longer afraid. Death would not be the end. Somehow, his spirit *would* continue in the Great Void beyond Life. The pain of disembowelment would be a minor price to enter the intriguing realm awaiting his spirit.

"Tomarinasai!" a deep-throated voice commanded him to halt.

Tomi's arms froze when he recognized the voice of Lord Fumio. He lowered the sword to the floor, confident he could once more pick it up and do what honor and duty dictated. He pivoted on one knee to face Fumio-*sama* and bowed deeply, his head touching the woven mat.

"What is this?" Fumio demanded. His stout, heavily muscled body filled the doorway, the voluminous sleeves of his kimono flapped as he folded his arms on his broad chest. "You could commit *seppuku* in my home without my permission? What causes such rudeness from the son of my great friend Tanaka Nobunara?"

"I have dishonored you, great sir," Tomi replied, his forehead still placed to the floor. "And I have disgraced my father and the family of Tanaka, of which I am no longer worthy to be a part. I have taken liberties with your favored concubine. I have abused your hospitality

43

and must forfeit my life to atone for my unforgivable conduct. Please grant me permission to commit *seppuku* so my debt to you will be paid and my ancestors will be appeased. Then may my soul find fullfillment in the Great Void."

Fumio-*sama* threw back his head and laughed. "Ah, young samurai! Your sense of honor does justice to your father and the name of Tanaka. Yet, I cannot grant you permission to commit *seppuku* for you have not violated my hospitality, but merely complied with my wishes.

"Do you not recall that I asked you if you found Mikko-*san* fair? When you replied in an affirmative manner, I commanded her to bring you to her chambers and treat you to the delights a woman can offer a worthy knight-warrior. I would have been offended had you refused. The sake has robbed you of your memory, fine samurai," Fumio declared. "Now raise your head from the floor and put your *ho-tachi* in its place. The time has not come for your death, Tanaka Tomi Ichimara, but when that time arrives, you will indeed die as a samurai!"

Since that night in Fumio-*sama's* palace, Tanaka Tomi Ichimara, later known as Tanaka Tom Fletcher, had faced death many times. Once he had again been prepared to commit *seppuku*, but there was no fear involved when he'd readied himself to plunge the blade into his intestines. Tom had never forgotten the lesson of that night or lost his conviction that Death is only a door from Life to a new existence.

"Tom?" Amanda Sommer's voice sliced through the memories. "Tom, you feel all right? You sure got a strange look in your eyes."

"I am fine," he grinned drunkenly. "I am a fine young samurai."

"Is that so?" she smiled. "Well, you sure look fine to me, and that's a fact."

Through whiskey-blurred eyes, Tom discovered they had entered a bedroom, equipped with a feminine bureau and mirror, gayly designed wallpaper, framed paintings, and belongings suited to a woman of the West. Amanda guided him to a four-poster bed. The samurai felt himself sink into the soft mattress.

"You're the first honest-to-goodness hero we've ever had in Marzo Viento," Amanda said as she unfastened the hooks and buttons of her long satin dress. "You'd like as not have a big marble statue put up in your honor if the folks around here could manage it."

"My horse and mule," he muttered. "I must see to their care. *Bajutsu* demands it."

"Who in tarnation is Bah Jitsue? You ain't married to an Indian are you?"

He stared at her sharply. How could she know about Paloma, the beautiful Apache woman of the Valbajo Tribe in Arizona? Paloma had regarded herself as his wife and he had come to think of her as a favored concubine, not unlike Lord Fumio's Mikko-*san*. He'd left Paloma with child. His child.

"Oh, hell," Amanda shrugged. "Don't matter to me no how. You appear to be part Indian yourself and that don't bother me none."

"My horse, my supplies . . ."

"Calm down, Tom," she urged. "Jacob is takin' care of your critters free of charge and I had Bart bring your gear up here. See? I got it in that corner. Got everything there except all that gold and money. Arnold Dell took that to the bank. He'll keep it safe for you 'cause he'd be afraid to do otherwise. You oughtta be more careful with all that loot."

"I have had too much rice wine," he commented thickly.

"Rice wine?" Amanda laughed. "That's about the only thing you *didn't* have tonight."

45

"I have been careless," he muttered. "I must not do so again. It is not wise. It is not samurai."

"What's this samurai thing?" she asked. "Oh, never mind. All that doesn't matter now."

Her dress fell to the floor and she began to unfasten her undergarments. Tanaka Tom pulled his *katana* and *ho-tachi* from his *obi* and placed them near the bed. Despite his drunkenness, he felt his loins stir at the sight of Amanda removing her clothing. Soon the woman stood completely naked. Tom appraised her full breasts and finely curved torso with appreciation. The hips flared and tapered into long shapely thighs and legs. He smiled at the triangle of red hair—the Chamber of Pleasure—between her thighs.

"Come and undress me," he instructed.

"Can't you manage?" she asked, slowly crossing the room to join him on the bed.

"You shall undress me as one unwraps a fine gift," he replied, his deft fingers plucking at her erect nipples.

"You got a mighty high opinion of yourself," she remarked, her annoyance vanishing as his skilled touch increased her longing.

"The gift will be for both of us," he assured her, gently kissing her throat. "The union of a man and a woman. Nature's greatest pleasure risen to the summit of ecstasy."

His lips moved steadily until they stimulated the base of her neck. Tom's hands stroked her breasts and thighs simultaneously. Amanda's body trembled with desire. She'd never been so aroused by foreplay. Tanaka Tom Fletcher might be an odd character, but he seemed to know more about pleasing a woman than any man she'd known before.

"Guess it's Christmastide," she whispered and eagerly reached forward to unbutton Tom's trousers.

* * *

The Six-gun Samurai had enjoyed the limelight of the town's hero-worship and many favors—especially Amanda's. However, the following morning he prepared to leave Marzo Viento. His reason for coming to New Mexico had died at the hands of Wilkins and his men. The death of Eddie Mears meant Tom would have to find another lead to Hollister and the other members of the 251st Ohio.

Amanda had left him alone in the room to fetch their breakfast. He assumed the knock at the door would be her returning with the tray, but Tom's hand dropped to the handle of the *katana* in his sash. Last night he had been careless. His conduct had been unbecoming a warrior-knight of *Dai Nippon*. He vowed never to forget he was a samurai and that he would never compromise his status by excess liquor again.

"Hal Newton, Mister Fletcher," the sheriff's voice announced. "Mind if I talk to you a spell?"

"Please enter, Sheriff," Tom invited.

The lawman stepped into the room, pushing the door shut behind him. "You fixin' to leave town?"

"I have completed my business here," the samurai nodded.

"You couldn't maybe reconsider, could you?" Newton asked awkwardly. "I'm in a helluva mess right now and I could sorely use your help."

"Yesterday you saved my life, Sheriff—"

"Hal."

"Hal," Tom nodded again. "For that I am in your debt. If it is in my power to assist you, I shall do so gladly."

"Well, let me explain what the situation is before you go committin' yourself," the sheriff urged. "You see, that feller we locked up yesterday, the young bandido you hit with this thing," he extracted the blood-stained *shuriken* from his belt and handed it to the samurai.

"Turns out his name is Carlos Alverez. If you know who Fidel Alverez is you'll know how important that is. He's better known as El Halcón."

"My Spanish is somewhat less than fluent," Tom admitted. "*El Halcón* means 'The Hawk,' yes?"

Newton nodded. "But the hawk I'm talkin' about is a wild son of a bitch that heads the meanest bandido gang in the entire Southwest. Alverez used to be an officer in the Bolivian Army, so he's managed to whip his boys into an efficient fightin' force that can ride and shoot like they was veterans of Jeb Stuart," he sighed heavily. "Well, little Carlos claims he's El Halcón's kid brother."

"And you are afraid that these bandits will come for him?"

"Oh, they will," Newton said grimly. "El Halcón isn't gonna fret none about ridin' into a little town like this. He and his men will take Marzo Viento apart and there ain't much I can do to stop him. In fact, I kinda doubt there's much *anybody* can do against him unless we got about half the U.S. Cavalry to lend a hand."

"But you want me to try?"

"Jeremy Pike was killed yesterday. The job of deputy is open. No man in town is willin' to accept it. I'm askin' you to put on a badge and join me. Like I said, I didn't want you to commit yourself until you knew exactly what you'd be up against. Now you do, and I'll accept your answer and understand if you ride out of here as soon as you can saddle your horse and load your gear."

"I am obliged to you for saving my life, Hal," Tom began. "But nothing in life occurs in a haphazard manner. My karma has led me here. Even when I discovered that the man I was seeking had been killed, Fate still steered me to Marzo Viento in search of my swords and other belongings. Now honor and duty urge me to remain. This too is my karma."

Sheriff Newton stared at him, utterly bewildered by the samurai's statement. Tom smiled. "Yes, Hal," he said. "I shall accept your offer and be your deputy, although I know nothing of such work. I shall remain in Marzo Viento until El Halcón and his men are no longer a threat to this town."

"I just hope we all live long enough to see that day," Newton replied grimly.

Five

Tanaka Tom Fletcher emerged from the sheriff's office, his swords in his *obi,* .45 Colt on his left hip and a copper badge pinned to his kimono jacket. He stepped onto the plankwalk and walked to the barber shop beside the jailhouse. The legend on the sign posted above the entrance made the samurai smile.

SHAVES   HAIRCUTS   HOT BATHS

All three, especially the latter, appealed to Tom. He entered the barber shop and bowed politely to the nervous and frail Burl Davidson. The barber stared at the badge on Tom's chest and swallowed hard, his Adam's apple protruding under his chin like a loose marble.

"Morning, Mister Fletcher . . . er, Deputy?" Burl stammered. "What can I do for you today, sir?"

"I desire a bath and your services as a barber," the samurai answered.

"Oh, well, sure thing, Deputy," Burl nodded eagerly. He moved to the back door and opened it. Clem Porter sat on an apple crate behind the shop. The drunkard had built a small campfire under a tin can filled with water, grass, and bits of food he'd collected from table scraps, which he stirred slowly with a stick. "Clem, heat up some water for *Deputy* Fletcher double quick!"

"Yessir, Mister Davidson," the drunk replied. He abandoned the poorly concocted "soup" and rushed inside.

"The water will take a little while, Deputy," Burl explained. "Why don't you just sit right here and I'll clip your hair just like you wants it done." The barber smiled weakly, his watery eyes betraying his apprehension to Tom's presence.

Clem placed a metal bucket on a flat-topped stove and fed kindling into its belly to increase the flames. Tanaka Tom placed his *katana* in a corner near the barber chair before he sat down. He put the *ho-tachi* short sword on his lap. Burl trembled as he draped a long white cloth over the samurai's chest, covering him to the knee. The barber reminded Tom of a praying mantis with the soul of a rabbit.

"Now, let's take a look at what you got for me to work on," Burl said timidly, raising Tom's rice-reed hat. "And I'll . . ."

Davidson stared in amazement at his customer's head. He had never seen a samurai topknot before, the hair combed straight back on his skull, held in place by a gold clasp, and the pate shaved on both sides of the summit. Burl had once seen a picture of a Mohawk Indian with a single column of hair running acsoss the center of an otherwise bald head, but he'd never heard of anyone who favored a hairstyle similiar to this incredible stranger who'd wandered into Marzo Viento and now wore a lawman's star.

"What . . . whad'ya want me to *do* with it?" the barber asked numbly. "That is, with your hair, Mister Deputy?"

"Hair stubbles are growing around my topknot, yes?" Tom replied sharply. Since this man dealt with

51

people's hair, such a thing should be obvious. "Shave the stubbles away and trim the hair. I repeat: *Trim* it. If it continues to grow, it will resemble a Chinese queue, which I do not want. But I will be most angry if you cut it without care."

"I understand, sir," Burl answered, wishing he did.

"Water's heatin' up, Mister Davidson," Clem stated.

"So start filling the deputy's tub, you whisky-soaked ol' fool!" the barber snapped. "Can't you see I'm busy?"

The town drunk grinned impishly. He understood why Burl was trying to bully him. The newcomer terrified him and he lashed out verbally at Clem to try to ease his own tension. So long as Porter received his three cents for preparing the bathwater and sweeping out the shop, Burl could yell to his heart's content.

The barber stirred his brush in its cup to prepare the shaving soap. "Reckon it'll be nice weather today, Deputy?" he inquired. His voice seemed almost desperate.

"We must accept whatever the elements bring," Tom replied flatly. He wondered why this man asked so many foolish questions.

"Guess you're right, sir," Burl agreed. He gingerly dabbed lather on one side of the samurai's head and prayed the formidable customer would be satisfied with the results of his efforts.

The door opened abruptly, the frame slapping into the wall so hard it was a wonder the glass didn't break. Tanaka Tom recognized the rat-face of the dust-covered, leanly muscled man who entered. He recalled Clay Young's sadistic smile when he'd watched Eddie Mears's violent death in the arroyo the day before. Clay swaggered into the barber shop and hooked his thumbs in his gunbelt. The familiar cruel grin appeared on his narrow face. A short, thickly built cowboy followed at his heels. The samurai recognized him as another one of Mears's killers.

"Have a seat, gentlemen," Burl invited, but his voice trembled worse than ever and his shaky fingers threatened to drop the straight-razor from his hand. "There's another chair outside. Just haul it in and . . ."

"We didn't come in here so we could practice waitin'," Clay snickered. "Me and Art done rode all the way from the Big W spread so we could get all shaved and prettied up for the party Old Man Wilkins is havin'."

"Gonna be a real rip-snorter," Art Moore chuckled. "We're bringin' a bunch of greaser girls so everybody can have a good time."

"So we wanna look nice and be smellin' sweet as fresh tanned leather when we meet the ladies," Clay added.

"I'll be happy to oblige just as soon as I take care of Mister Fletcher," Burl assured him.

"Fletcher?" Clay smiled, revealing even more ugly teeth. "I don't recollect seein' him before."

"Don't reckon you'd be apt to forget a funny-lookin' jasper like him either," Art chuckled.

"Hold on a minute," Clay urged. "Maybe it ain't this feller's fault he got such a sissy hairdo."

Tom glared angrily at the cowobys, who slowly approached the barber's chair. Burl Davidson cowered away from them, his eyes expanding to fill the lenses of his wire-rimmed glasses. Clem moved behind the inadequate shelter of the tin bathtub in the backroom. Clay folded his arms akimbo on his narrow chest and gazed contemptuously at the samurai.

"Did Burl get liquored up and do that to you, Mister?" he asked.

"Maybe some redskins tried to scalp him and only got half the job done," Art suggested mockingly.

"Mister Fletcher is the new deputy," Burl told them, hoping to discourage further harassment.

"You're joshin', ain't you?" Clay snorted. "Hell, even that ol' fool Newton wouldn't deputize a goddamn half-breed what wears his hair like some kind'a she-boy!"

"Reckon he's wearin' a skirt under that there sheet?" Art nudged his friend with an elbow.

"Don't appear to be," Clay glanced at Tom's trouser-clad legs. "But I ain't gonna believe he's no lawman until I see his badge."

"So why don't we take a peek?"

Art reached forward and seized the sheet tucked under Tanaka Tom's chin. He smiled and tightened his fingers on the cloth. The cowboy jerked the sheet away from Tom's torso. A samurai battle cry filled the barber shop and a flash of silver lightning sent Art Moore reeling across the room.

Tom's *ho-tachi* had slashed the cowpuncher's denim shirt from waist to throat. Severed buttons clattered to the floor. Art Moore and Clay Young stared in horrified astonishment at the polished steel blade of the samurai's short sword. Art threw both hands to his bared chest, expecting to feel blood pouring from a long, ghastly wound. To his relief, he discovered only cloth had been cut by the sword stroke.

"Jesus," Art whispered, dazed by his startled emotions.

"You loco son of a shit-eatin' dog!" Clay snarled. He unfolded his arms and dropped his hand to his holstered .44 Colt.

Tom's *ho-tachi* moved faster. The samurai had already sprung from the barber's chair and swung his sword down in a blur of motion too fast for any man's eye to follow. Clay cried out, surprised by Tom's incredible speed. He felt something tug hard at his right hip an instant before his hand groped for the walnut grips of his sidearm.

Clay's fingers closed on fear-chilled air. The Colt revolver—still sheathed in its leather holster—lay at his feet. The samurai had sliced it off the cowboy's gunbelt before he could draw the weapon.

Art recovered from his shock and grabbed for his Smith & Wesson. Tom's .45 Colt seemed to fill his left hand as if by wizardry. The cowboy stared into the black muzzle of the deputy's revolver and threw both hands overhead in surrender.

"I am Tanaka Tom Fletcher," the lawman announced coldly. "The hair that you make sport of is worn in the traditional manner of the samurai warrior-knights of *Dai Nippon*. You shall honor it or remain silent concerning it, but never mock me again. I am also a bona-fide officer of the law as long as I wear this badge and you are creating an annoyance that reflects badly on my professional ability if I allow you to continue. Do you understand?"

Clay and Art woodenly nodded in reply.

"Now go," Tom snapped. "Your unwashed presence offends me. I do not wish to smell your stench while the barber attends to my hair."

"The deputy is gonna take a bath afterward too," Clem Porter announced cheerfully. Burl glared at him fearful the drunkard would make matters worse, but Clem's wide grin didn't fade.

"Even *you*," the samurai began, addressing Clay and Art. "Should be civilized enough to allow a man to bathe in peace."

"Yeah," Art said quickly. "That'd be downright un-neighborly."

The paunchy cowboy staggered out the door. Clay Young, however, sneered at Tanaka Tom. "You might find that badge to be too big a burden for you to handle."

Then he turned and stomped from the shop.

* * *

55

"What the hell is the matter with you, Tom?" Sheriff Newton demanded. He banged a fist on his battered desk hard enough to jar the blue tin coffee cup, nearly spilling the contents on a pile of wanted posters.

"Nothing," the samurai replied as he entered the sheriff's office. "I am in fine health."

"I heard about that ruckus you caused at the barber shop about an hour ago," Newton declared. "If I hadn't been at Jeremy Pike's funeral, I would have known about it as soon as it happened. Christ, Tom! The barber shop is right next to this office!"

"Why does that matter? The incident that has alarmed you must concern the two uncouth louts that accosted me, yes?"

"Of course that's what I'm talking about!" the sheriff replied with exasperation in his voice. "You pulled one of those swords of yours and assaulted them!"

"If I had done that, they would be dead," the samurai stated simply. "I merely cut one man's clothing and prevented the other from drawing his gun. He did not lose a single fingernail, so I would hardly call it an assault."

"But you shouldn't have done it at all!"

"They were rude," Tom declared. "If they behaved in such a disrespectful manner in Japan, I would have been within my right as a samurai and a warlord fourth-class to execute them."

"You ain't no warlord in this country."

"I am what I am anywhere I happen to be," Tom sighed. "Considering the circumstances, I feel I acted with great restraint."

"*Restraint?*" Newton's eyes bulged. "You pull that toad-sticker . . ." He pointed at Tom's long sword.

"This is a *katana* and would never be dishonored in the practice of lancing toads," the samurai told him. "Besides, I used my *ho-tachi*."

56

"Damnit, Tom! It doesn't matter which one you used. You can't go around slashing a sword at folks for half a reason. And—in the United States, a feller being rude isn't enough reason to use a weapon on him."

"Duels are still fought in this country, yes?" Tom asked. "Is not one reason for this because one man has offended the other's honor?"

"How did those two dumb cowhands offend you?"

"They insulted my hair."

"What?" Newton wasn't certain he'd heard Tom correctly. His statement didn't make any sense to the sheriff.

Tanaka Tom doffed his rice-reed hat to display his bare head. Newton stared at the topknot and shaven pate with disbelief. "I wear my hair in the traditional manner of a samurai knight-warrior. It is my right and my duty to retain this practice."

"What you wanna do with your hair is your business, Tom," the sheriff assured him, choosing his words carefully. "But that looks . . . mighty strange to somebody brought up to Western ways."

"That does not matter."

"It matters if'n you're gonna cut up somebody for makin' unflatterin' remarks about it."

"They have no right to insult me or my samurai traditions!"

"You figure it's worth all the trouble and possible bloodshed when you could just adopt another way of wearin' your hair instead?"

"I cannot!" Tom insisted. "I am a samurai and my topknot is a symbol of my rank and a matter of my warrior heritage!"

"Is that a fact?" Newton smiled thinly. "Well, those Levi trousers you're wearin' and that Colt revolver on your hip *ain't* part of your samurai culture, is it? You got yourself a Western saddle and a Winchester in the boot. Where's that fit into your Japanese traditions?"

"For an American you know much of the samurai," Tom commented, an eyebrow raised in wonderment.

"Just what I've read about 'em," the sheriff answered. "Came across a story about Commodore Perry's voyage to Japan in a newspaper . . . hell, must'a been almost twenty years ago. Anyway, it mentioned the fearless, sword-wieldin' warrior-class that were so obedient to their masters, they'd cut themselves open if commanded to do so. Reckon I found the samurai pretty intriguin'. Whenever I happened upon anythin' about you fellers—which didn't happen very often—I studied on it and sort'a filed it away in my memory. Sure never figured I'd actually meet a samurai, that's for sure."

Tom smiled, impressed by Newton's intelligence and desire to learn. The sheriff's formal education may have been slight, but his thirst for knowledge and natural curiosity had expanded his worldliness beyond the level one might expect of a lawman in a tiny border town in the New Mexico Territory.

"Your observations have merit, Hal," he admitted, mentally pushing aside his samurai pride. "Adopting certain clothing and equipment has proved advantageous to me in this country. Yet, I am not prepared to compromise my topknot in a similar manner."

"You're gonna have to change a lot of your traditions in this country unless you want a whole hell of a lot of trouble every time you take off your hat," Newton shrugged. "You say that hairdo is a symbol of your rank as a samurai. Well, here nobody is gonna know what the blue blazes that topknot of yours means and the fact you're a samurai back in Japan don't give you any special authority in the United States. You want a symbol of authority folks around here will understand? That badge you're wearin' is it."

Newton leaned back in his chair and formed a cradle for the back of his head with his interlaced fingers.

"Authority always carries responsibility with it. Reckon one way or the other there's a price for everythin' in life. In Japan, your samurai rank means you're responsible for your actions, right? You gotta follow orders from your warlords and whatever else you've got over there. If your boss tells you to rip your belly open, you gotta do it. Well, as long as you're wearin' that tin star, you've got certain responsibilities as well. You're obliged to keep the peace in this town, but that don't give you no special right to bully folks or use unwarranted force."

"These responsibilities are not easy to obey," Tom sighed. "But I have never failed my duty as a samurai. As I am in your debt, you are, to a degree, my *daimyo*. I will comply with your wishes as much as my honor can tolerate."

"What about your hair?"

"I must consider that very carefully before I decide whether to retain my topknot or abandon it," the samurai answered glumly.

"So long as you don't pull no swords because of it, I don't much care," Newton commented. "Better keep your hat on as much as you can. By the way, since you're a white man, how'd you become a samurai in the first place?"

"I was on the ship with the Commodore Perry you spoke of. The American mission was attacked and I fled into the heart of Edo. I might have died in that crowded city if a samurai had not adopted me as his son."

"You must not have been very old back then."

"No. I was only twelve, but old enough to serve as a midshipman."

"Well, didn't your folks back in America wonder about what happened to you?"

"I don't know if they were ever informed of my whereabouts or new life in Japan."

59

"Then you haven't seen them since you came back?"

"I have returned because of them," Tom replied grimly. "I seek the men of the 251st Ohio Regiment. They murdered my family in Georgia and I am duty bound by the code of *bushido* to avenge this wrong."

"That sounds almost like Matt Wilkins's way of thinkin'."

"Wilkins?" Tom knitted his eyebrows. "Those two troublemakers at the barber shop work for this Wilkins, yes?"

"Along with a couple of dozen other fellers," the sheriff nodded. "Luckily, some of his staff are old servants and womenfolk, but he still has a lot of young fellers with lots of honker blood in their veins. Clay Young is about as nasty as he's got, but he ain't the only hardcase on Wilkins's payroll."

"How did they get Eddie Mears?" Tom asked.

Newton blinked with surprise. "You know about that?"

"Mears belonged to the 251st Ohio," Tom explained. "When I learned he was being held in your jail in Marzo Viento, I came to extract information concerning the location of my principal enemy—Colonel Edward Hollister."

"You told me earlier that the man you were huntin' had been killed," the sheriff recalled. "Would that be Mears? You saw Wilkins kill him?"

"Yes," Tom shrugged. "I also heard Wilkins say that Mears had stolen his cattle. If this is true, the rancher was acting accordingly, so it is not important."

"Like hell it ain't!" Newton exclaimed. "If Wilkins had caught Mears stealin' cows on his property and either shot him or strung the little bastard up from the nearest cottonwood strong enough to hold him, I'd say he'd be more or less within his rights. But Mears had been arrested by Jeremy and me and we was holdin' him for his trial. Although I personally got no doubts a'tall that Mears was guilty, even a guilty feller has a right to a fair trial and a legal execution. He's also got a right to protection while he's waitin' on that trial. Matt Wilkins has always been sort'a impatient, but we didn't figure he'd ride in here with his men, hold us at gunpoint and haul Eddie Mears out of his cell. Knew for sure that boy was as good as dead when they dragged him out'a town."

"He is dead," Tom confirmed. "But that incident is over. Wilkins did what he thought was right, just as you and your deputy tried to do as your duty and laws required. It was karma that the rancher seize and execute Mears."

"Mears ain't what concerns me," Newton told him. "I told you already that we've got El Halcón's kid brother locked up in that cell back there. Well, Fidel Alverez and his gang hit the Wilkins ranch a couple'a months ago. They vandalized his house, killed a few old house servants and they raped and murdered his wife and daughter."

Tom nodded, sympathizing with Wilkins's loss.

"Now we already know what Matt Wilkins was willin' to do to get his hands on a feller that stole a few of his cows," Newton sighed. "It ain't hard to guess what he's gonna want to do when he finds out we have little Carlos held prisoner."

"Wilkins's family has been destroyed. He is bound by honor to revenge, just as I am committed to my *bushido* vengeance."

"Jesus, Mary, and Joseph!" Newton exclaimed. "Don't *you* side with him, for crissake! Me and *you* are bound to uphold the law and the Constitution of the United States of America. That means we don't let Wilkins take Carlos Alverez outta that cell, no matter how much we agree with his notions about personal justification."

"His vengeance is justified," Tom insisted. "I would do no less in his place."

"The Alverez kid is gonna hang," Newton declared. "Half this town saw him rob the bank and gun down Jeremy. When the circuit judge arrives, that sonufabitch will get a fair trial, but he'll be found guilty for sure. When that happens, old man Wilkins can slip the noose over Carlos's head and pull the lever to the trapdoor of the gallows if he likes, but he'll have to wait 'til *after* Alverez is found guilty in court. He's our prisoner and he's under our protection as well as our confinement. Wilkins ain't gonna take him, unless it's over our dead bodies."

"A condition that would not stop me if I were Wilkins," Tom replied grimly.

Six

Fidel Alverez sighed while Pepe Ortega diligently swept the hard bristled brush over the sleeves of his black shirt. Ridiculous practice, the bandido chief thought. Yet, he had conceived the idea of El Halcón, the bird of prey that walked like a man and fought like a devil from hell. The Hawk who swooped down on his victims and struck without mercy with metal talons. Such a campaign of terrorism requires certain symbols. El Halcón always wore black. It was his badge of rank among his followers, it told superstitious *peónes* that the powers of Darkness rode with the bandido gang, and it was a constant annoyance when dust settled on his clothing.

"Your uniform of battle is now ready, *Don* Fidel," Pepe declared. "Would you like me to prepare some *té* now?"

The bandit chief smiled. Pepe Ortega had been a servant of the Alverez family in Bolivia. He had served El Halcón's father until Francisco Alverez's death and he'd loyaly remained with the son as his personal valet and trusted friend—perhaps the bandido's only friend.

"*Gracias,* Pepe," El Halcón replied. "But I shall wait until my return to enjoy some tea. The less one has in his bladder while on horseback, the better."

"Of course, *Don* Fidel," the white-haired servant nodded. Sadness was etched into Pepe's wrinkled features. An old man with a stooped back and aching joints, his life had been dedicated to attending to the needs of others. He'd cared for the property of his masters while possessing little himself. He'd helped Francisco Alverez raise a family while all but abandoning his responsibilities to his own wife and children.

El Halcón gently placed a hand on Pepe's shoulder. "You should leave, my friend," he said softly. "You are too old for this kind of life. I would give you enough money to find a home elsewhere."

A thin smile appeared on the servant's face. "Where would I go, *Don* Fidel?"

"Mexico is not far. Perhaps Texas."

"I know no one in those places," the old man replied. "I have served no one except your family. I have done so for too long to do otherwise."

"You should go, Pepe."

"No," the valet shook his head. "My place is with you. Since you have chosen the way of the hill bandit, my place is here, in your camp."

"You do not approve of what I do?" El Halcón inquired, although he knew the answer. Pepe had never told him, since a proper servant does not criticize his master, but Alverez knew.

"It is not for me to approve or condemn your decisions, *Don* Fidel," the old man stated. "But I would not be unhappy if you changed your occupation to some-

"I will," the bandido promised. "One day I will be thing less dangerous and more peaceful."

able to give up this violent trade. The Alverez family will have a great *rancho* with a fine *hacienda* as in the old days. I will marry and have strong sons and beauti-

64

ful daughters. Even my wild brother will one day mature enough to seek these things as well. We will raise cattle or sugar cane or tobacco," he smiled. "And I will have many servants with you in charge of them. When that time comes, Pepe, you will never work again. You'll merely see that others are not loafing and then sit on the porch and bask in the sun until it is time for you to sleep in your own feather bed."

Pepe allowed the dream to form briefly in his mind's eye, although he did not believe any of it would ever materialize. "We shall still play chess in the evenings after I've seen that the cooks prepare your supper and the table is set?" he asked, forcing the corners of his mouth to rise.

"Of course we will, my dear friend," El Halcón assured him. "It will be the very best for all of us."

"I shall look forward to those days, *Don* Fidel," the old man replied as convincingly as possible.

"Now, I must go," Alverez declared. He buckled his gunbelt around his narrow waist. Six-foot-two, El Halcón was a tall, slender man with raven black hair and a trimmed mustache. Clad in his black uniform, his appearance created an atmosphere of formidable power. He slipped the rawhide retaining loop over the hammer of his holstered Remington revolver and inserted the cords of his *bolas* into his belt.

"I pray you will be safe, *Don* Fidel," Pepe said.

"Do not worry," El Halcón replied. "When my brother returns, tell him I wish to have some words with him about his conduct. Carlos and the four men that left the camp without permission will all be restricted to this area until I can decide a proper punishment for them."

"*If* Carlos returns, *Don* Fidel," the old man said softly.

"I am also concerned about his safety," Alverez admitted. "He is young and occasionally foolish, but he is not stupid. He will not try to confront more than he can deal with."

"He thinks, with the arrogant mind of youth, that he can deal with far more than he is truly able," Pepe remarked.

El Halcón nodded in grim agreement. Carlos had become rebellious to his brother's authority and his behavior had grown increasingly reckless. Still, worry would not protect him. Perhaps it would be best if Carlos did not return.

The thought made Fidel Alverez's mind recoil in horror. To hope for the loss of his last living relative was foul and selfish. He promised himself to say *"Ave Maria, graciana Dominus"* a hundred times when he returned from raiding the village the bandits had found to the South.

El Halcón emerged from his tent. Other canvas structures were positioned in a circle around the camp. His men, forty-three seasoned bandidos, stood by their horses. A more ruthless, vicious collection of cutthroats never existed in the Southwestern United States than Alverez's gang. Most of them were Mexicans and former members of other less successful bands. A few were half-breeds turned renegade to strike out at a world that refused to accept them as equals. Two ex-slaves had joined the gang, hoping to punish the white race and make a profit in the process. Only one American Caucasian had ever belonged to El Halcón's troops. He had been murdered, his throat slit while he slept, by one or more of his fellow outlaws.

Alverez scanned his men with less than pride in their appearance or their personalities. Most of them seldom washed or groomed themselves in any way. Their manners were loud and obnoxious, yet they had proved to be fierce if not courageous in battle. They feared and respected their leader and generally followed orders without question. El Halcón realized that they obeyed him because his raids had always been successful and fruitful. If he failed to lead them to victory they would turn on him like a pack of rabid dogs. One unprofitable operation could be enough to trigger a bloody mutiny.

"You all know where we are going and what to do," the bandit chief announced. "You should all be prepared for today's engagement."

A sea of wolfish grins on dirty, bearded faces told him they were.

"Mount your horses," he commanded.

A chorus of cheers replied to his order. The bandidos climbed into their saddles as Juan Ruiz, Alverez's second in command, brought the leader's big black stallion forward. El Halcón mounted his horse.

"*¡Vámanos!*" he shouted.

The bandits galloped from the camp gleefully. Pepe Ortega stepped from his master's tent and watched the riders disappear from view, squinting his eyes amid the fog of dust caused by numerous rapid hooves.

"*Vaya con Dios,*" the old man whispered, but he knew God would have little reason to go with Fidel Alverez that day.

The village was small and quiet, with a population of two dozen farmers with their families. It basically functioned as a commune, each unit supplying what goods he manufactured or grew to his neighbors in return for other goods and services. Everyone worked hard and shared fairly equally—except the family of Ramon Moreno.

A large, grossly fat man, *Don* Ramon, as he insisted the villagers address him, had once been a bandido in Mexico. When the *federales* captured him, he managed to convince them to spare him by leading them to the lair of his compatriots. In return for his betrayal, Moreno was permitted to take his three sons—also bandits—and leave the country unharmed. Moving to the United States, the Morenos discovered a safer, if less astronomically profitable, method of survival.

They lured poor *peónes* to join their farming community. Each family received three acres of land, but in return for this property, the fruits of their labor would be supervised by the Morenos. They were also promised protection, supplied by the Morenos—who took great pains to be certain they owned the only firearms in the village.

Ramon and his sons soon had the docile *peónes* under their figurative thumb. They assigned the villagers to whatever tasks they desired. The Morenos helped themselves to the best of their subjects' goods and selected whatever attractive young girls appealed to them for their lustful pleasure. Resistance was dealt with harshly. Occasionally, the former *bandidos* delivered a beating or two, but they hadn't felt it necessary to "execute" any of the villagers for almost a year. The *peónes* accepted their fate and did not attempt to rebel against the *patrón* and his offspring. After all, they were unfamiliar with violence and the Morenos had all the guns.

The *patrón* scratched at the fleas in his beard while he watched the farmers hoe their gardens. Perhaps being a petty dictator of a small *aldea* was not as rewarding as robbing gringo banks, but it had its satisfactions and pleasures and the only risk involved concerned the lack of tequila and beer that threatened to make existence in the future rather bland.

At forty-eight, Ramon didn't feel much need for excitement anyway. He was settled in a community that he ruled like a feudal lord. The old bandit days no longer appealed to him and he hoped his sons felt the same. Ramon loved his three vicious offspring and didn't want them subjected to the hazards of their former occupation.

68

"Papa," Luis, his eldest son, said, descending the steps of an adobe church. "I seen about ten men on horseback, heading this way from the east."

"*Mexicanos* or gringos?" the senior Moreno inquired, drawing his tarnished old Walker Colt revolver from its holster. He wondered if the damn thing would even fire. He hadn't used it for years.

"I could not tell, Papa," Luis replied. "What should we do?"

"Fetch Geraldo and Jesus. Tell them to arm themselves in case our visitors are looking for trouble."

"Ten men are too many to fight . . ."

"You boys have more than ten bullets in those fancy rifles of yours, no?" Ramon snapped. "So get yourselves into position and wait. Maybe these men aren't nothing but a group of lost *vaqueros* from a cattle drive or something, but if they are more than that, you be ready or you might lose your Papa."

"Sí," Luis nodded nervously. "We will be ready."

The three sons moved quickly to the sturdiest buildings in the village. Luis returned to the church, Jesus knelt by a window inside the Moreno house and Geraldo stationed himself within the communal barn containing the village pigs, cows, and goats. They fed shells into the tublar magazines of their Henry carbines and prayed to a God none of them really believed in for protection for their beloved father. Ramon shuffled his obese body to the door of the church. If any shooting occurred, even he should be able to retreat within the adobe structure in time to avoid injury.

All eyes turned to the ten approaching figures on horseback. Ramon knew they were in trouble when he saw the crossed *bandoliers* on many of the rider's chests. An old bandido recognizes his own kind at a glance. His eyes threatened to burst from their sockets when he spotted the tall man mounted on the black stallion leading the group. El Halcón himself!

The riders entered the village and leisurely rode to the church. They were aware that every eye followed their progress and that three gun muzzles were trained on them. El Halcón brought his mount to a halt. The others followed his example.

"*Buenas dias*, Ramon," Alverez greeted. "How are you this fine afternoon?"

"You know of me, *Señor*?" Moreno replied, his voice betraying his fear.

"Sí," El Halcon nodded. "I never go *anywhere* unless I know something about the people. You have made a good life for yourself here, no?"

"We are a poor village, *Señor*," Ramon answered. "If we can accommodate you in anyway, it will be my pleasure, but surely you would do better to . . . visit a rich gringo ranch instead."

"You are not being inhospitable, are you?" Alverez demanded coldly.

"Oh, no!" Moreno assured him. "Stay if you like, but we have little to offer you and your men."

"Food is not a little thing, Ramon," the bandit chief commented. "You have women and my men have not enjoyed a lady's company for almost a month. That is a long time for a man with Latin blood in his veins, no?"

"Oh, sí!" the fat ex-bandit laughed nervously. The hard expressions on the faces of the riders warned him that El Halcón had not been joking. Ramon fell silent.

"And, I think maybe you have some gold too," Alverez remarked. His cold smile resembled a grinning skull.

"We are a poor village . . ." Ramon began.

El Halcón shook his head. "Ah, Ramon. Do you not know that it is a bad thing to die with a lie on your lips?"

Moreno's terror was intensified by a high-pitched scream from the communal barn—where Geraldo was hidden. He nearly tripped as he charged into the adobe

70

church, expecting to feel bullets crash into his broad back when a volley of gunshots exploded from El Halcón's gang. Ramon sighed with relief even as his terrified heart hammered uncontrollably within his flabby chest. Then he realized none of the shots had been aimed at him.

The bandidos had fired directly at the bell tower. Several rifle shots from men who'd crept into the village from other directions, accompanied the pistol reports of the ten outlaws on horseback. Luis Moreno didn't live long enough to fire his Henry. The bullet-riddled body of the boy toppled from the tower and fell in a bloodied broken heap before El Halcón and his bandits.

Ramon heard the brass bell above chime furiously and guessed what had happened. His sons! They had killed Geraldo and Luis and probably Jesus as well. Anger and grief mingled with his fear. He placed his back flat against the adobe wall and tried to clear his muddled mind to determine what to do next.

A snarling voice suddenly filled the church. Ramon turned to see a hunched figure charge forward from the pews, a rifle held in his firm grasp. He barely saw the flash of the bayonet fixed to the weapon's barrel before he felt the sharp steel point slam into his chest. Hot agony coursed through his nervous system. In the flickering of an eye, he understood what had happened. El Halcón und his nine riders had served as a distraction while others crept surreptitiously into the village. This bitter knowledge was his last earthly thought. His pierced heart ceased to function and he died.

"Save ammunition," El Halcón ordered as he dismounted. "Don't shoot unless you must."

The other bandits cheered. Many appeared from their hiding places throughout the village, bearing rifles with fixed bayonets. Others knelt by their horses and attached the deadly blades to the barrels of their guns.

Peónes wailed fearfully. Men, women, and children ran in all directions in a vain effort to escape their fate.

Some of the farmers stood in stunned horror and allowed themselves to be run through by charging bayonets. Others fell to their knees and begged for mercy. Grinning *bandidos* replied by thrusting cold steel into the *peónes'* chests or throats. Most fled. Bandits on horseback overtook most of them and clubbed the frightened villagers with rifle stocks. They shoved blades into the unconscious men and draped the women over their saddles to return them to the center of the community.

Two *peónes,* a man and a woman, managed to outrun a fat bandit on an equally out-of-shape and undersized mustang. Rifle shots brought the villagers down. Another *peón* fled to the barn in the hope of retrieving Geraldo's Henry carbine.

El Halcón spun his *bolas* overhead, judged the distance between himself and the farmer, and released the Bolivian weapon. The cords of the *bolas* struck the *peón's* neck, the lead-filled balls whirling in a violent revolution before slamming into the victim's skull with bone-crushing force.

Accustomed to tryanny, few of the *peónes* tried to fight the invaders. Yet, seeing their children and the older, less attractive women slaughtered, inspired enough rage to motivate four farmers into an effort of self-defense.

One man tried to bring the blade of his hoe down on Juan Ruiz's head. The wiry bandit blocked the descending shaft of the tool and promptly butt-stroked the farmer in the face. The *peón* fell and Ruiz drove his bayonet into the victim's intestines and jerked the blade upward until it connected with his breastbone. El Halcón drew a machete from a sheath attached to his saddle and moved forward to confront two furious *peónes*.

A sickle-wielding farmer tried to slash open the bandit leader's face while his partner lunged with a pitchfork. Alverez deftly side-stepped the sickle blade and slammed the edge of his jungle knife into the man's midsection. The heavy machete cleaved through flesh and muscle to destroy the *peón's* stomach. He crumbled to the ground, blood and partially digested food spilling from the ghastly wound.

The pitchfork-armed farmer attacked again. El Halcón's jungle knife clanged against the metal tines, deflecting the thrust. Suddenly, the bandit's leg kicked high, his razor-sharp spur slashing into his opponent's face. The *peón* screamed and dropped his improvised weapon. Blood oozed from his ravaged cheek and sliced eyeball. El Halcón's machete struck again, chopping into the side of the farmer's neck, nearly decapitating him.

Lonny Phillips, a muscular black bandit, nearly laughed aloud when the fourth *peón* attacked him with just his bare hands. Lonny swung his rifle overhead and brought the walnut stock down hard, cracking the fury-driven farmer's skull like an eggshell. Pink and gray brains dripped down the man's face as he wilted to the ground.

The dying *peónes* moaned pitifully until the final bayonet thrusts terminated their agony. El Halcón discovered an old man lying on his back, his shirt stained red from a poorly aimed stab to the chest. Alverez placed a booted foot beside the injured man's head and sharply dragged a spur across the *peón's* throat. Blood gushed from the severed carotid and jugular. The old man's body contorted wildly in the dust before Death claimed it. Soon only the sound of weeping women and laughing bandidos remained.

"We have fifteen women," Lazaro Morales, brother of the late Pedro, reported happily. "All young enough to please a man and old enough to know how."

"Juan," El Halcón told his second in command. "You have first choice of the women. The rest of you decide peaceably which man gets which woman and in what order. Don't quarrel. You'll all get your chance."

"My brother will be sorry he was not here today," Lazaro grinned.

"So will mine," Alverez smiled. "Enjoy yourselves. I'm going to search Moreno's house for whatever treasures the old bastard had tucked away."

"Don't you want none of these sweet young things?" Lonny Phillips inquired.

"The Hawk has a dove waiting for him," the bandit leader replied proudly. "With such a woman at my beck and call, to have sex with any other would be as senseless as masturbation."

El Halcón marched toward the home of Ramon Moreno as Lazaro called out, "Are we going to take the women back to the camp with us?"

"No," Alverez replied, glancing over his shoulder. "There isn't enough room or food for them. Besides, I don't trust these women. A few of the male curs had enough courage to fight. Perhaps a few of the bitches will have a taste for vengeance as well. Kill them when you're finished."

"Sí," Lazaro muttered with regret.

Seven

Tom spent most of the day learning his duties as Hal Newton's deputy. The sheriff explained how to patrol the streets after dark and stressed the importance of checking the doors of closed business buildings to be certain they were secure.

"If somebody wants to leave his home unlocked, that's pretty much his risk," Newton explained. "But if he left his place of business that way, he probably done it by accident. The best way to keep folks honest is to make temptation difficult."

"Then I should inform the store owner that he did not secure his property?" Tom asked.

The sheriff nodded. "But it ain't likely you'll find any unlocked doors in Marzo Viento after sundown. Folks here are real good at keepin' outta trouble."

"Hmmm!" the samurai grunted. "None of them seemed eager to get involved in the trouble yesterday."

"That's a fact," Newton agreed. "You ain't gonna find much excess courage around this town. I suspect Amanda Sommer has more backbone than any man in Marzo Viento. Oscar Brill doesn't seem to have a yellow streak, but he's indifferent as hell and a full-time sonofabitch. I reckon the reason he remains in this little town is because nobody here has enough guts to punch him in the mouth when he gets snotty. Maybe it's a good thing nobody tries. Brill never goes anywhere without that Remington of his and I figure he don't just wear it for a decoration."

"If El Halcón comes for his brother, we will need all the help we can get."

"Don't count on none from the people here, Tom," the sheriff warned. "I don't know quite how these folks got to be the way they are. Maybe it's because some of their families headin' West lookin' for gold found nothin' but hardship. A few lost loved ones due to Indian raids or outlaws. I hear that's what turned Clem Porter into a drunk. Anyway, I guess folks just wanted to live somewhere peaceable."

"A worthy goal for men that are not warriors by birth or occupation," Tom remarked. "But the only way to retain peace is to be willing to fight for it."

"Sounds like a contradiction."

"It is not," the samurai insisted. "I have seen other towns and communities that wished to live in peace, and I've seen men like El Halcón who wanted their property. The only way to deal with such men is by violence. The alternative is to surrender to the invading tyrant's will. Then one will have neither peace nor freedom—except the ultimate release of cares in this lifetime found in the grave."

"I'm inclined to agree with you, Tom," Newton assured him. "But tryin' to get folks in Marzo Viento to fight ain't gonna be easy."

He explained basic law and various town ordinances to Tom and urged the samurai to study the regulations of Marzo Viento and the Constitution of the United States. Tom examined the latter with interest. Many years ago as a child it had been impressed upon him that the articles and amendments of the Constitution were mandatory for the protection of the republic and America's freedom. He noticed three articles (the 13th, 14th, and 15th amendments) had been added to the document since his journey to Japan.

Tom recalled parts of the Constitution vividly and he'd seen evidence of its influence since returning to the United States. The freedom of religion kept the government from enforcing a favored faith on the citizens as the monarchs in Europe had once done. The freedom of speech and the press permitted the people to express themselves in a manner the ruling class of *Dai Nippon* would not have tolerated. Apparently the right of the people to keep and bear arms helped to insure their other freedoms. Tom wondered how long he would have survived if his American allies had not had access to firearms in the past.

He discovered Newton's claims concerning Carlos Alverez's right to a trial by jury. Articles five, six, and eight guaranteed the bandit's right to a fair trial and protected him from cruel or unusual punishment or an impromptu execution before he had been legally found guilty. The samurai frowned. So many privileges for one suspected of a crime did not sit well with his aristocratic Japanese sense of justice. Then he recalled that twice he had been arrested and the same laws had applied to him. Tom read a sentence in the 6th amendment that pleased him.

"It says here that the accused should have a swift and public trial," he told the sheriff. "Why don't we have the trial now, in the street to be certain the proceedings are public? Then, when Carlos is found guilty, we shall execute him and have done with it."

"Hell, Tom," Newton muttered. "That wouldn't be no fair trial. The folks in this town would hardly comprise an impartial jury. We'll have to wait for the circuit judge to arrive and see to the legal proceedings. The jury will probably be made up of other folks that live in the district but weren't witness to the bank robbery or Jeremy's murder. Besides, having the townspeople try the little bastard might backfire. If they figure El Halcón will leave Marzo Viento be if they let the kid go free, they might be scared enough to find him innocent."

"Perhaps you're right," Tom agreed. "In article eight, I notice that it forbids cruel and unusual punishment. Does this include torturing a prisoner to gain information? If we knew where El Halcón was located we might be able to attack him first and solve our problem by direct action."

"Torture?" Newton stared at the samurai. "Hell no, you can't torture a prisoner!"

"*I* would not," Tanaka Tom replied. "It would be beneath my dignity as a samurai. Only lowly born individuals serve as torturers."

"People aren't tortured in this country."

"But I have seen it. The Valbajo Apaches used such methods and I witnessed floggings in San Francisco and a place called New Cannaland in Colorado."

"The Apaches got their own laws and whatever you saw those white men doin' with a whip was probably illegal. Just cause somethin' is against the law doesn't mean everyone obeys it."

"True," Tom nodded. "Otherwise there would be no need to have lawmen, yes?"

"Or samurai," the sheriff smiled.

Tanaka Tom shook his head. "There will always be need for samurai. We are more than warriors. We are part of the Japanese culture. The samurai keeps traditions from dying. We are guardians of the past and beacons to the future."

"How do you figure that?"

"The future has its roots in a people's history. If the past is forgotten, the present withers and the years to come will be without culture, and civilization itself shall perish."

"I reckon so," Newton shrugged, confused by the samurai's explanation. "I just hope you know how to handle that six-gun as well as you do a sword or a bow and arrow."

"I was trained with the weapons of the Japanese elite for many years before I acquired my skill with firearms," Tom replied. "Yet the principles of martial arts apply to all weapons. A gun is aimed like a bow. The bullet is a projectile, not unlike an arrow or a *shuriken*. The fast draw of a *katana* is similar to rapidly bringing a pistol to play."

"I don't really understand what the hell you're talking about," Newton sighed. "But I guess you do and that's what matters."

The samurai nodded in agreement.

Tanaka Tom Fletcher completed his rounds that evening. Hal Newton suggested he get some sleep before his next watch at three in the morning. The samurai retired to the Sommer House Saloon, but he didn't plan to sleep immediately. Amanda Sommer eagerly obliged when Tom told her to follow him upstairs.

They made love for nearly three hours. Without the depressive effect of excess alcohol to dull their senses, both partners performed to the peak of their sexual ability. Their naked bodies coated by a film of perspiration, Tom and Amanda lay pleasantly exhausted, on her bed.

"I ain't never met a man that knew so much about how to please a woman," she remarked, deftly rolling a cigarette and licking it down. "How'd you learn so good?"

"A woman's needs are not unlike a man's, but there are subtle differences," he answered. "A man wants to feel proud of his trade and a woman desires pride in her femininity. A man finds satisfaction in his accomplishments, but a woman's accomplishments are based on how she pleases her man."

"Your opinions ain't exactly accurate," Amanda said dryly. "I'll have you know runnin' this saloon is quite an accomplishment and . . ."

Tom kissed her neck slowly and gently traced his tongue along the sensitive mastoid region behind her ear. Amanda trembled and purred with pleasure. She tossed the unlit cigarette to the floor and turned to her lover.

"One more time, Tom? Please?" she urged.

"That's the other secret to satisfying a woman," the samurai smiled.

"What's that?" Amanda asked in a puzzled voice.

"Endurance," he whispered, drawing her into his arms.

The sudden reports of pistol shots interrupted their love-making. Tom disengaged from Amanda's embrace and ignored her squeals of protest. He hurried to the window. Peering outside, he saw three men on horseback in the street below. They shouted unintelligible sounds of joy and fired their weapons into the air. The samurai frowned.

Amanda joined him by the window. "Oh, hell," she said. "That's just a couple of Matt Wilkins's boys come into town to do a little Saturday night hell raisin'. Figured they'd all be at that party the old man was havin' tonight, but I reckon it got too dull for them three."

"But they are disturbing the peace, yes?" Tom remarked. "There is a law against such behavior. I must stop them."

"They're just lettin' off some steam," Amanda shrugged. "You can't go out there and shoot them just for that, and since there's three of them and only one'a you, there ain't no other way you're gonna quiet 'em down."

"They are breaking the law," the samurai insisted, pulling on his trousers. "Besides, they are rude."

Disregarding Amanda's pleas to forget the trio of rowdy cowboys, Tom buckled his gunbelt around his waist and slid the *ho-tachi* short sword into it. He didn't bother to don his shirt or boots. Opening the door, he dashed into the corridor and ran to the stairs. He bounded down three steps at a time in his bare feet. The customers in the saloon had cowered away from the entrance, fearful of the indiscriminate shooting in the street. Only Oscar Brill, who sat alone at a table in a corner playing solitaire and sipping whisky, and Clem Porter seemed unconcerned by the incident.

The town drunk liked Saturday nights because he went to the Sommer Place Saloon and earned drinks by cleaning up after careless patrons. Occasionally someone would buy him a beer. Sometimes the "generous" soul demanded Clem "earn" it by getting on his hands and knees and barking like a dog or eating some sawdust from the floor to prove he really needed the drink. Clem's pride had been destroyed by grief and alcohol long ago, so he always agreed to perform no matter how humiliating the act might be. He was busy sweeping up a broken beer mug when the shooting occurred and barely noticed Wilkins's men outside.

"Let me see your broom," Tom's voice commanded.

Clem turned, wondering what the speaker would want him to do in return for a free beer. He didn't recognize the samurai at first glance since Tom's well-muscled torso appeared fuller and more powerful without clothing. Clem held his broom forward, confused by the request. Steel flashed as the *ho-tachi* whirled from its scabbard. The sharp edge struck the shaft of the tool just above the bristles. Even Porter's liquor-soaked mind reacted to this unexpected action. He cried out in alarm and released the broom to stagger away from the samurai.

. "Thank you," Tom said, snatching the stick before it could fall and quickly sliding the short sword back into its scabbard.

The samurai ran the broom through his hands, testing its weight and length. It was shorter than the forty-inch *maru-bo* fighting staff he had used in Japan, but the stick was more than an inch thick and made of sturdy hickory. Tom's instructor in *bojutsu* had been Donchi Ken, who'd studied under the great Akahachi Oyakei in Okinawa.

The batwings swung open. Clay Young, Art Moore and a lanky, bearded cowhand named Josh Spencer entered. All three men had holstered their revolvers before they dismounted and headed into the saloon. Clay displayed his ugly teeth with a wide smile.

"Get the best whisky out," he ordered. "We's gonna howl tonight!"

Clay Young howled—in pain. Tanaka delivered a *tsuki-komi,* both hands locked around the broomstick as he drove one end into the cowboy's solar plexus. Clay's eyes bulged and his breath spewed from him like a deflated balloon. He wilted to the sawdust-covered floor in a wretching, moaning heap.

"Oh, no!" Art exclaimed before Tom pivoted and smashed the stocky cowboy in the jaw with a *gyaku yoko uchi* blow that butt-stroked Art into Josh Spencer.

Both men fell back through the batwings. Art landed on his back, dazed by the samurai's attack. Josh stumbled into the street, but kept his balance and rapidly dragged his Navy Colt from its holster.

Tom had followed his opponents outside and immediately responded to Josh's threat by bringing the staff down on the cowboy's wrist. The Colt dropped from numb fingers. The samurai dropped to one knee to compensate for the shortness of his stick and delivered a *gedan uchi* low stroke to Josh's ankle. The blow swept the startled man off his feet and sent him sprawling into the dust.

Still stunned and flat on his back, Art reached for his Smith & Wesson. Tom rose and stamped the butt of his *bo* stick into the cowboy's flabby gut, just above the groin. Art Moore rasped, convulsed violently, and flopped on his belly to vomit.

Josh Spencer climbed to his feet and charged the samurai, determined to take the broomstick away from him. Tom's staff slapped into Josh's forearms, deflecting his groping fingers. The samurai executed a *morote uchi* stroke, his fists holding the stick in a horizontal position to thrust the hickory staff under the aggressor's jaw. Josh Spencer's teeth clashed together painfully and an explosion of light burst inside his head before he surrendered to unconsciousness and crumbled to the ground.

Tom looked down at his vanquished opponents with satisfaction. The sound of a revolver hammer cocking back dispelled his pleased emotions. Clay Young still clutched his sore midsection as he staggered through the batwings and leveled his .44 Colt at the samurai.

"Pretty fancy fightin'," he hissed through clenched teeth. "But that piece o' wood ain't gonna stop no bullet!"

"Don't do it, Clay!" Bart Finely, the bartender urged. "He's the deputy!"

"I don't give a shit if'n he's the president of the United States," the cowboy replied.

"But he saved the bank from being robbed," Joel Stewart, the cobbler declared. "And he helped capture El Halcón's kid brother!"

Clay's mouth opened in awe. He glanced over his shoulder and stared at Joel. "You tellin' me they got that bandido bastard's kin over in the jailhouse?"

"That's right, Clay," Bart confirmed. "You don't wantta kill the feller responsible for that, do you?"

"I reckon not," the cowhand smiled, despite his pain. "Leastwise, not just yet."

He eased the hammer of his Colt forward. Sheriff Hal Newton jogged from the law office, his Greener shotgun held ready. "What's going on?" he demanded.

"Your deputy just earned hisself a ree-preeve," Clay replied, sliding his revolver back into its leather. "Mister Wilkins might not take kindly to me killin' the man that caught El Halcón's brother."

"They were disturbing the peace, Hal," Tom explained. "I stopped them."

"Yeah," Newton groaned. "I noticed."

"Do we put them in jail?"

"No need for that," Clay assured him. "Me and the boys will ride out peacefullike."

Art Moore slowly rose to his hands and knees and Josh Spencer moaned as consciousness dimly returned. Clay helped both men to their feet and assisted them onto the backs of their horses. He mounted his own sorrel and grinned at the lawmen.

"Much obliged for the information, fellers," he stated, touching the brim of his hat. "I'll see you later, Deputy. Like I said, this is just a ree-preeve."

"Yes," Tom agreed. "A reprieve for *you*."

The cowboy scowled, but didn't reply. The three men applied spurs to their horses and galloped from the town. Newton shook his head grimly.

"We're gonna have trouble from Matt Wilkins," the sheriff declared. "Big trouble."

Eight

Tanaka Tom Fletcher followed Sheriff Newton back into his office. Newton placed his shotgun on the desk and sank into the chair behind it. The samurai closed the door and placed the broomstick in a corner.

"Did I deal with them correctly for disturbing the peace?" he asked.

"You might have asked them to stop before you beat the hell out of them," the sheriff shrugged. "Right now my main concern is what Wilkins is gonna do when he finds out we've got little Carlos locked up."

"Despite what your Constitution says," Tom said, "can we not release him to the rancher? It is his right to avenge the murder of his family."

"Tom, this ain't Japan. Our laws and morality are different."

"Morality differs little from one culture to the next. All civilizations acknowledge that murder and stealing are wrong. None condone adultery or bearing false witness against others."

"This is a Christian nation," Newton told him. "We don't advocate takin' the law into your own hands. People here, for example, think suicide is wrong while in Japan you were taught that it's honorable to cut yourself open if your warlord orders you to do it."

"Ah!" Tom's face lit up. "A Christian nation, yes? I have not read the Bible since I was a child, but does it not include a passage . . ."

"Don't bother to tell me that *'Thou shalt not kill'* line," Newton sighed. "Since Moses, David, Samson, and a bunch of others did a whole lot of killin', it's obvious that means *'Thou shalt not murder.'* "

"True, too obvious to discuss," Tom agreed. "And it would have little to do with our conversation. No, I refer to the passage in the Book of Numbers that provides for the right of family members to avenge their murdered loved ones."

"Hell, I don't remember nothin' like that," the sheriff shrugged. He opened a drawer and removed a battered Holy Bible. "Numbers you say?"

Tom nodded.

Newton turned up the flame of the kerosine lamp on his desk and thumbed through the Bible until he found the passage. "Here it is. Numbers thirty-five: verse nineteen: *'The avenger of blood shall himself put the murderer to death; when he meets him, he shall put him to death.'* "

"This *avenger of blood* is the family of the slain, yes?" Tom inquired. "And since the Bible is the holy book of your Christian nation, you should obey its laws."

"The Constitution is the guide for our laws in the United States," the sheriff insisted. "The Bible also says, *'Thou shalt not suffer a witch to live.'* Now, a lot of folks would figure that'd mean we should go around killin' every Indian medicine man we could find. That'd cause the worse redskin wars you ever thought of. And, like I said before, it's fine with me if Wilkins wants to kill Carlos Alverez *after* he's stood trial, but by God, he

86

ain't gonna take another one of my prisoners before the feller is even found guilty in court."

"Hmmm," Tom nodded. "That should satisfy both your Constitution and your Bible."

"But will it satisfy Matt Wilkins?" Newton wondered, his voice reflected his doubts.

"It may or it may not," the samurai shrugged. "You have conceived of the best solution to the problem. That is all a man can do. Deal with each situation to the best of his ability. How events unfold is in the hands of karma and we must live with that and continue to do our best."

"I ain't so sure Wilkins will *let us live* at all if we stand between him and his revenge."

"Life and Death are the same," Tom replied. "A man lives as he must and he accepts his death with honor."

The Six-gun Samurai returned to Amanda Sommer's room, made love to her once more and slept until Sheriff Newton rapped on the door and told him it was time to make his rounds. Tanaka Tom had walked many patrols in Japan and accepted the task in the disciplined manner of a samurai.

In *Dai Nippon*, he had defended his *daimyos* and the shogun himself from a host of enemies. Rival warlords might launch an attack with entire samurai armies, mercenary *ronin* swordsmen—samurai without a master—or *ninja* espionage agents. The latter were the most fearsome threat, especially when the darkness of night concealed the highly skilled *genin* (the *ninja* agents commanded by *chunin* subleaders who in turn operated under the orders of the *jonin* in control of the *ninja* clan) while they infiltrated the *daimyo's* defenses.

Tom had first encountered *ninja* as a child when they attacked the American mission, but his most vivid memory of them concerned one winter's day near the city of Koga. Tanaka Nobunara, Tomi Ichimara's adopted father, had been placed in command of a unit escorting the shogun's son to a meeting with *Daimyo* Yumio Saito. Thirteen years old and yet to receive the full honors of samurai rank, young Tomi was not privilege to the reason for this meeting, although he accompanied the escort force since Nobunara had decided the experience would be beneficial to the boy's training and understanding of a samurai's duties.

Marching through ankle-deep snow, most of the samurai were on foot, their *tabi* split-toed sandals reinforced by silk wrappings. Tanaka Nobunara and several other higher-ranking warrior-knights rode on horseback, while the shogun's honored offspring was carried in an ornate sedan.

The *ninja* agents struck before any of the escort saw the attackers. One of the samurai screamed when the double-bladed knife of a *kyoketsu-shogi* attached to a ten-foot cord, whirled into his exposed throat. The *ninja* wielding the weapon had materialized from the snow less than seven feet from the escort.

More *ninja* seemed to appear from nowhere, dressed in all-white uniforms complete with face scarfs and bladed *tabi* for walking on ice, instead of their traditional black garments for night fighting and infiltration. A rain of *shurikens* and needlelike *tonki* dropped half a dozen samurai before the attackers drew their swords (shorter than *katanas*, but slightly longer than *hotachis*) from white scabbards and charged.

Samurai archers fired their *take* bows, killing several *ninja*, but the agents were too close for the long range weapons to be used effectively. Tom saw a *ninja* parry a samurai's thrust with a *yari* spear and then close in to drive a dagger into the warrior's chest. Another *ninja* hurled blinding powder into the faces of four escorts and cut down two of them with his sword before a *ka-*

tana stroke decapitated him. One *ninja* blocked a sword stroke with his own blade and ripped open the attacking samurai's belly with a kick, using the spikes attached to his sandals.

A dying samurai, his throat torn by metal claws strapped to a *ninja's* hand, fell against Tomi, knocking the boy to the snow-covered ground. Armed only with the *tanto* knife tucked in his *obi*, Tomi desperately groped for his puny weapon as the white-clad killer leaned over him. The *ninja* drew back his arm, aiming the blades of his *shuko* "tiger claws" at the boy's sprawling form.

Suddenly, a bolt of blazing light struck the would-be assassin in the collarbone from behind, slicing diagonally to his breastbone. The *ninja's* scream was muffled by his face mask. Blood poured from the wound, splattering the terrified boy. Tanaka Nobunara pulled the blade of his *katana* from the lifeless *ninja* agent. His expression of concern for his adopted son turned into a smile of relief as he saw Tomi was unhurt. Nobunara quickly assumed a stern expression.

"It is true the battle is won," he stated. "But this is not the time to rest. On your feet, my son."

Due to this and other experiences with the stealthful, superbly conditioned *ninja* and fanatically dedicated enemy samurai, Tanaka Tom Fletcher did not take guard duty lightly. He remained keenly alert as he walked the shadowy streets until the pale sun appeared on the eastern horizon.

The samurai admired the dawn with the eye of a man raised in *Dai Nippon*. The Japanese are possibly the most color conscious people in the world and extremely sensitive to the subtle beauty of nature's paintbrush upon the sky. Tanaka Tom viewed the soft morning sun with appreciation as it slowly cast a gentle light that gradually engulfed the pale, cloudless sky. Venus, the morning star, shone brightly in the distance and the

89

half-moon had yet to surrender to the domination of day. Slowly it would retreat and await the dusk to return as master of the night.

Tom considered composing a haiku, but decided to postpone the poem. His duty to Sheriff Newton was his first priority and the pleasure of a morning cup of tea competed strongly with the enjoyment of watching the sky unfold its perennial drama.

The samuari entered the sheriff's office and gently closed the door. Hal Newton snored softly as he slept on a bunk in one of the cells. Carlos Alverez, who had been too frightened by his confinement to be an unruly prisoner, was already awake and seated on his cot. The young bandido had been certain his brother would come to his rescue when he had been captured, but his first night behind bars had robbed him of his confidence. His former arrogance, drowned by fear, he stared into the office at the deputy. The crude bandage on his wounded cheek did not diminish the dismay formed by his expression, yet resentment and hatred slowly altered his features at the sight of the man most responsible for his arrest.

Tanaka Tom removed a container of *cha* leaves to prepare some tea. He frowned when he noticed the supply was steadily dwindling. Although he had more *cha* in his gear stored within Amanda Sommer's room, that too would vanish if he used it too liberally. Regretfully, he put the tea away. Although coffee was a poor substitute to Tom's Japanese-acquired taste, it would have to do.

"*Señor*," Carlos whispered. "I do not know your name, *Señor*."

"Then you have not listened, for it has been spoken many times in this room," the samurai replied flatly.

"Listen," the bandido began, forcing a smile that caused his wounded face to smart. "I hit you on the

90

trail and you hit me outside the bank. I took your belongings and you take them back and get to see me in this jail. We even, no?"

"Correct," Tom nodded. The youth smiled broadly until Tom explained. "*No, we are not even.*"

"What's wrong with you, *Señor*?" Carlos demanded. "You wanna die maybe? That's what's gonna happen if you keep me in this cell. My brother, El Halcón, he's coming and he kill everybody here if you don't set me free. You fight pretty good, but El Halcón is the best of all. You let me go and I see that you are rewarded for helping Carlos. *¿Comprendé?*"

"You stole my swords," the samurai told him. "Nothing can compensate for that. You dishonored me, but I also dishonored myself by allowing a jackal pup like you to ambush me. For that reason, I shall be content with the knowledge that your life will be taken from you soon, even if I do not have the pleasure of killing you myself." He shrugged. "Your life is worth too little for me to have much interest in it."

"What is your own life worth?" Carlos hissed. "Never mind," he sighed. "I have heard you talk about death as if it was a trip to the next county. I think you must be *loco*. I only hope I get to see you die and find out if you are as brave as you think you are."

"You would not recognize courage," Tom smiled mildly. "As you have none of your own."

The sound of hoofbeats drew the samurai's attention to the street. The horses outside did not gallop, but the muted roar caused by their number told him many riders had arrived. He cautiously opened the door and peered into the street.

Men on horseback shuffled their mounts into position throughout the town. Although Tom could see less than a dozen, he guessed there were more, strategically stationed to cover every door and window in Marzo

91

Viento. Most of the riders were dirty and clad in dusty clothing with ammunition belts draped over their torsos and ill-treated sombreros on their heads. Four horses stood before the sheriff's office. The tall sinister figure of El Halcón, mounted on his black stallion in front of the other bandidos, waited near the door.

"Who is it?" Hal Newton asked, fully awake, his shotgun in his fists. "Wilkins?"

"No," Tom replied. "Remain here and watch the prisoner. The bandits have the town surrounded and they may try to slip Carlos a gun through the window of his cell. Be careful they don't take advantage of such openings to fire at you."

"What do you think you're going to do?" the sheriff demanded.

The samurai answered by opening the door wide and stepping onto the plankwalk to face the bandido gang.

"*Buenas días,*" Fidel Alverez greeted without warmth. "From what my fat friend Rodriguez tells me, you must be the man that does not die so easy and uses a bow and arrow like *El Diablo.*"

"I am called Tanaka Tom Fletcher," the samurai told him, bowing formally.

"I admire a fighting man. Even if he is fighting against me," the bandit chief declared. The other members of the gang glanced from Tom to their leader, noticing how similar the two men were. They both stood tall, were leanly built, with striking black hair and dark hard eyes. Their faces revealed the pride of aristocratic warriors. "You know who I am, *Señor* Fletcher?"

The samurai nodded.

"Then you know why I am here," El Halcón remarked. "My men and I could tear this town apart. Kill everybody. It wouldn't be much trouble, but it would be harder than raiding some village and I'd probably lose a few men in the process. I don't like to lose my men unless there is enough to make it worth the loss of a life or two. The bank is small and the people of Marzo Viento are not rich. I know this as I know about all places that concern El Halcón. The only thing you have that is of value to me is my brother, Carlos. Return him and I will forget that three of my men were killed here. El Halcón will not return if you do this. I give you my word. The word of one fighting man to another."

"I can not release him," Tom told the bandit. "I am bound by honor to see you do not take him."

"Sí," Alverez nodded. "You now wear a badge. That means you are pledged to protect this town, but there will be no town if you do not give me Carlos. Has there not been enough killing, *Señor*?"

"Killing is part of a warrior's trade," Tom shrugged. Suddenly, his left hand swept the .45 Colt from its hip holster. The hammer cocked back as the muzzle gaped up at El Halcón.

Alverez appeared surprised, but not afraid. The other bandits voiced alarm and groped at their weapons. Several guns aimed at the samurai, but Tom didn't remove his revolver from its threatening position. El Halcón leaned forward in the saddle, resting an arm across the horn.

"You disappoint me, *Señor*. Such rash and foolish action is more befitting my brother than a man like you. Are you eager to die? If so, you will soon get your wish."

"I am not eager, but I am not afraid," the samurai told him. "If I die, I shall be reborn to an honorable new life."

"Is that so?" El Halcón raised an eyebrow. "You sound quite certain of your strange beliefs, *Señor* Fletcher."

"I am," Tom confirmed. "Just as I am certain that I can kill you even if your men shoot me first."

"Death is something every fighting man comes to accept with little terror," Alverez shrugged. "Maybe we die together, eh?"

"Sheriff," the samurai called out. "Do you have your shotgun aimed at Carlos Alverez?"

Newton realized what Tom was doing. "Sure do," the lawman replied. "First shot I hear, I'll let him have both barrels too!"

El Halcón's expression hardened. "You spoke of honor. What honor is there in killing an unarmed boy locked in a jail cell?"

"My vow to keep him from falling into your hands will be kept," the samurai announced. "Your men may destroy this town. They may kill everyone here. Yet you will not win."

"Neither will you, *Señor*," Alverez replied coldly.

"I will only lose my life," Tom said. "You will lose your life and know that what you came for is also lost."

A shrewd judge of character, El Halcón realized the strange deputy's threat was genuine. "So, our first game of chess is a stalemate, *Señor*," he smiled thinly. "There will be another game, another time—a time that will be better for me."

He pulled the reins of his horse to steer the animal away from the building. The other bandidos followed their leader's example. Alverez glanced over his shoulder at the samurai.

"Then, I will kill you, *Señor* Fletcher," he declared.

The bandits broke into a fast gallop and rode from Marzo Viento.

Nine

Carlos Alverez laughed, the sound combining relief with near hysteria. He gripped the cell bars and threw back his head as he wailed like a hyena in a zoo. The dust slowly settled in the streets while Tanaka Tom waited to be certain the bandidos had not regrouped in the distance to launch a full attack on the town.

The samurai didn't really expect such a tactic by El Halcón because it would endanger his brother's life, even if it would give the bandidos the element of surprise. Fidel Alverez would bide his time before he returned, but Tom felt certain the deadly chess game El Halcón had mentioned would continue and his opponent would prove to be a skilled and experienced player.

"I thought we was gonna be a couple'a customers for ol' Oscar Brill," Hal Newton sighed, stepping to the doorway. "You handled that damned good, Tom."

"I understand how El Halcón thinks," the samurai replied thoughtfully. "There was no fear in his eyes, only determination. The others are thieves and brutes, but their leader is indeed a warrior. We must not underestimate him."

"Didn't figure anybody was," the sheriff commented dryly. "Reckon he'll be back today?"

"We must assume he will strike at any time."

"Then we'd better walk patrol in the day as well," Newton said. "Generally I just stroll through town when I feel like it, but I figure we can't afford to be casual with things as they are."

Tom nodded in agreement. "When do you want me to make my next rounds?"

"Around noon," the senior lawman answered. "You'd better get something to eat and maybe grab a couple more hours sleep," he grinned. "You do *sleep* occasionally when you're in Amanda Sommer's bed?"

The samurai smiled. "It is most relaxing," he replied simply.

Tanaka Tom followed the sheriff's advice. He ate a light meal, as was his custom, and returned to the Sommer Place Saloon. Amanda was busy supervising preparations for reopening the tavern so the samurai slept alone in the bed. His philosophy of life and death, and his fatalistic belief in karma allowed him to drift into a tranquil slumber, unfettered by anxiety or fear about the uncertain future.

Newton rapped on the door at two in the afternoon, but Tom was already awake and fully dressed, his weapons donned in the usual manner. The samurai relieved the sheriff and assumed his duties of street patrol.

The citizens of Marzo Viento seldom seemed to set foot from their homes and places of business even in the warmth of day. Tom had never seen such a frightened town. Even the poor villages in Japan that lived in the fear of possible bandit attack—and the villagers were prohibited from owning weapons—did not contain the quality of trembling dread the samurai felt among the people of Marzo Viento.

The yellow-brown dog emerged from an alley. It

96

stopped, splay-legged and sniffed the air several feet from the unconcerned deputy. The scent triggered the animal's memory and warned it that this was not a man to be trifled with. Whining resentfully, the dog retreated into the alley rapidly.

"Howdy, Tanaka," Oscar Brill greeted. The undertaker sat in a straight-backed chair on the plankwalk of his shop. "Hot day, ain't it? Not fit for man nor mutt from the looks of it."

"You appear to be the only lover of fresh air in Marzo Viento," Tom mused. "The others seem to favor the indoors."

Brill chuckled. "Hell, Tanaka. You know as good as me that they're all shit-scared."

"But you are not?" Tom raised an eyebrow.

"Scared of what?" the mortician shrugged. "Dead folks is my business. Speakin' of which, you let me down last night, Tanaka. Figured you'd kill at least one of Wilkins's boys. When them bandidos rode in this mornin' I said to myself, 'Ol' Tanaka is gonna make me some business today and maybe add to it hisself,' but damned if you didn't disappoint me again."

"You saw El Halcón in the street, yet you did nothing?" the samurai's anger was restrained by fascination of the undertaker's cynical indifference.

"What was I supposed to do? Them fellers had my place surrounded just like everywhere else. The Hawk has his men well organized. Bet there was close to fifty of them."

"They were ready to destroy the town and kill everyone—including you," Tom explained. "Does that concern you?"

Alarm flickered across Brill's expression, but he soon vanquished it with a wide grin. "Why, hell no, Tanaka. I figured you'd protect us. The hero of Marzo Viento would take care of them fellers with his trusty bow and arrow or his swords and whatever else you use. A

97

bunch of bandidos with guns ain't no match for Tanaka the Great and his broomstick!"

The mortician laughed heartily at his own joke. The samurai felt tempted to force Brill's mocking words down his throat, but the sudden sound of shattering glass dismissed his interest in the mortician.

Crashing furniture and distressed voices echoed from the Sommer Place Saloon. Tom ran to the tavern. A chair lay in the street surrounded by glass fragments from a large broken window. The samurai expected to discover a tremendous brawl in progress as he pushed through the batwings. To his surprise, he found a single tall, muscular figure responsible for the commotion.

The burly cowboy hurled a half-empty whisky bottle into the mirror behind the bar. Glass exploded in all directions. Three male patrons of the saloon cowered into corners, their arms shielding their heads fearfully. Two men—the blacksmith, Jacob Fritter, and the bartender, Bart Finely—lay sprawled on the sawdust-laced floor. Amanda Sommer screamed at the towering vandal to stop, but he ignored her.

"You are under arrest," Tanaka Tom declared.

The big man turned slowly to face the samurai. He was six-foot-three and built like a bull buffalo. A smile pulled up the corners of his lips and his gray eyes flamed with amusement and lust for battle.

"You talkin' to me, Deputy?" he asked, a thick Irish accent flavoring his words.

Tom nodded. "You are disturbing the peace." He mentally leafed through other ordinances. "And you have destroyed private property and assaulted two citizens. I am taking you to jail. Come or I shall force you."

"Well, now," the big man said. "I don't guess I'd be likin' your jail very much, so I guess you'll have to force me a bit—if you're able."

"Careful, Tom!" Amanda warned. "That's Jethro Madigan. He's strong as an ox and meaner than a sidewinder. He pole-axed Bart and Jacob like they was a couple of puny kids."

"Ah," Madigan grinned. "But the deputy is carryin' a gun and a couple o' swords," he stretched his arms apart wide. "As you can see, I'm not armed, Deputy. I don't imagine you've got enough guts to take off all those fancy weapons of yours and try me man-to-man on my level, now would you?"

"Very well," the samurai agreed, unbuckling his gunbelt.

"Tom!" Amanda cried. "Don't do it!"

Tanaka Tom placed the holstered Colt on a nearby table and withdrew his *katana* and *ho-tachi*. Gently putting the honored samurai weapons with the gunbelt, he turned to see a ham-sized fist rocketing toward his face.

Tom pivoted, avoiding the punch and quickly seized the wrist behind the attacking hand. He slung his other arm around Madigan's triceps and bent his knees as he hauled the larger men onto his shoulder. The samurai straightened his legs and bent his waist, sending the startled Irishman hurtling over his back in an *ippon-seoi-nage* throw. Madigan crashed to the floor.

Eager to end the fight swiftly, Tom launched a kick at the mastoid behind his opponent's ear. Madigan was faster than his size indicated. The samurai's boot barely grazed the Irishman's hard skull before Madigan scrambled from the floor and charged Tom like an enraged bull.

The samurai chopped the side of his hand at the big man's neck, but the *shuto* stroke hit a well-muscled shoulder without effect. Before Tom could whip a bent knee into the aggressor, Madigan slammed into him. Tanaka Tom was lifted off his feet and suddenly found himself seated abruptly on a table. A rocky fist smashed into his jaw and and sent the samurai head over heels across the table to fall unceremoniously to the floor.

Madigan seized a chair and swung it overhead while the dazed deputy rose to his hands and knees. The Irishman brought the chair down with all his force, shattering the furniture when it struck the floor where Tom's head had been an instant before he jerked it aside.

The samurai jumped to his feet. Madigan slashed the broken backrest of the chair at Tom. The lawman weaved out of range, but the Irishman raised a booted foot and propelled it into Tom's chest. The blow knocked Tom backward until the small of his spine connected with the edge of the bar.

Madigan charged, stabbing one end of the improvised weapon at his opponent's face. Tom side-stepped deftly and the Irishman's belly slapped into the bar, his thrusting arms extending the wooden backrest across the counter.

The samurai stepped forward and drove his left elbow into Madigan's kidney, then whirled to hammer the bottom of his fist between the big man's shoulder blades. The Irishman howled with pain and dropped the piece of the chair. His hand seized a beer mug on the counter. He hurled his arm overhead and tossed the contents into the samurai's face.

Beer stung Tom's eyes and he staggered back two steps. Madigan's free hand back-fisted the deputy in the cheekbone and sent him into a table.

Madigan brought the mug down on the edge of the bar, shattering half of it. Tom blinked his eyes to clear them and saw the Irishman advance, holding the jagged glass like a deadly cestus.

"You fight pretty good, Mister Deputy," Madigan snarled. "Now, let's see what you had for breakfast!"

100

He punched the broken mug at Tom's face, but the Six-gun Samurai danced out of reach. Madigan executed a roundhouse slash. Tom side-stepped and launched a powerful *fumikomi* kick to his opponent's knee. The Irishman cried out as bone grated in the joint. The samurai grabbed Madigan's wrist with both hands, twisted hard and forced him to drop the jagged piece of mug. Tom's leg rose sharply and smashed the heel of his boot into the Irishman's mouth.

The kick straightened Madigan's back as blood oozed from his pulverized lips. Still holding the captive wrist in his left hand, Tom stooped to thrust his right arm between the larger man's legs. The samurai lifted Madigan onto his shoulder, carried him to the bar and hurled the stunned Irishman over the counter like a bale of hay.

Madigan crashed into what remained of the broken mirror and fell behind the bar. Incredibly, the powerful cowboy slowly rose, hobbling on his dislocated knee, his face and shirt stained with blood. He leaned heavily on the bar and stared at the samurai through blurry eyes.

"You're under arrest," Tom told him.

"Fuck you!" the Irishman replied, spitting red globs from his butchered lips.

The samurai's arm streaked out, his hand clenched in a *seiken* forefist. The big knuckles of the middle and index fingers connected with the point of Madigan's jaw like a butting ram. The big man's eyes rolled, his head snapped back and he sunk to the floor. This time he didn't get up.

"Jesus, Deputy." It was Joel Stewart, the stocky cobbler who'd cringed in a corner throughout the brawl. "I ain't never seen no fightin' like that. That some sort'a Indian wrestlin'? You was screamin' like a Commanche on the warpath."

Tom had been unaware of his *kiai* karate shouts during the battle. The cries increased his strength and concentrated his breath control while he was delivering each blow. Joel Stewart and the other Westerners in the saloon would not understand this principle of the martial arts, so Tom did not bother to explain.

"One of you help me drag this man to the jailhouse," he commanded.

Joel bobbed his head. "Yessir!"

Amanda moved closer to Tom and placed a cold, wet cloth to the corner of his mouth. The samurai was surprised to discover he was bleeding.

"I didn't figure nobody could best Jethro Madigan with his fists," she remarked with admiration. "Reckon I should have known better."

"Why did he do this?" Tanaka Tom asked, gesturing to indicate the shambles within the saloon.

"I got no idea," Amanda shrugged. "He just came in here and started bustin' the place up. Maybe his boss fired him."

"Oh?" the samurai raised an eyebrow. "Who does he work for?"

"He's one of Matt Wilkins's men."

"Ah," Tom whispered. "Now I understand!"

"Understand what?"

"How Mister Wilkins plans his revenge."

Ten

Matt Wilkins and four of his men rode into town later that afternoon. They dismounted in front of the sheriff's office. The rancher entered without knocking and found himself facing the Colt .45 in Tanaka Tom Fletcher's hand.

"Good manners are worth cultivating," the samurai told him, lowering the six-gun.

Wilkins was a tall man, nearly as tall as Tom. Exposure to the elements had tanned his deeply lined face. The gray sideburns extending beyond his white Stetson indicated the man had passed fifty, but his barrel chest and trim waist revealed he'd remained fit. The fierce blue eyes that peered from hooded lids provided further evidence of the rancher's toughness and determination.

"I didn't come here to discuss social niceties," he replied gruffly. "I take it you're the new deputy I heard so much about. You made quite an impression on the boys. Clay Young'd like to shoot you on sight while Art and Josh were too scared of you to come to town until I told them I'd fire any yellow son of a bitch who was afraid of a feller that beat up folks with a broomstick. None of them seemed to know your name though."

"I am Tanaka Tom Fletcher," the samurai answered.

"I'm Matt Wilkins."

"I know," Tom nodded. "I've seen you before."

"Don't recall us ever meetin', Fletcher." Wilkins tipped back the Stetson with a thumb. "Figure I'd remember a feller like you."

"I watched you and your men kill Eddie Mears," the samurai explained. "I did not consider it a prudent time to introduce myself."

"Is that a fact?" the rancher frowned. "Not that I doubt your word, but suppose you tell me what you saw."

"You and three other men dragged Mears until he was close to death. Then you shot him twice with a pistol. I believe Clay Young and the one called Art accompanied you. Mister Young seemed to enjoy himself that day."

"You was there all right," Wilkins growled. "Mears was a goddamn rustler. He stole my cattle and I punished him good and proper for it. Not gonna let no judge or town-bred jury let a bastard like that get off scot-free." The rancher produced the makings for a cigarette from his pocket. "You bury Mears, feller?"

"No."

"Good," Wilkins nodded, sprinkling tobacco into a curved piece of paper in his other hand. "His kind don't deserve no funeral."

"So you said," Tom commented.

The rancher raised his head. "Good eyes and good ears you've got, Fletcher. I hear you're mighty good with a whole lot of weapons too. Reckon I'll stick with shootin' irons myself." He rolled the cigarette and licked it down. "Since you're a lawman, I figure you don't take kindly to the way I handled that Mears owlhoot."

"It does not matter to me," the samurai shrugged. "It

was just that he died violently and who did it or why is not important. Mears was my enemy or at least he was associated with the men I have sworn to kill. I had hoped to question him to learn more of my foes' whereabouts, but karma dictated this was not to be."

"Who the hell is Carman?" Wilkins asked, scratching a Lucifer match to life on the top of Newton's desk. He held the flame to his cigarette and puffed gently.

"Karma," Tom smiled thinly. "It refers to destiny or fate. At least I was permitted to watch Mears die."

"Glad you enjoyed the show, Fletcher," Wilkins snorted smoke through his nostrils. "Did you happen to meet up with one of my boys today? Feller named Madigan?"

"He is residing in one of our cells, Mr. Wilkins."

"Figured that's what happened," the rancher growled. "At least you didn't kill him."

"I have not killed any of your men, although they have tried my patience."

"Mine too," Wilkins sighed. "All right. How much'll it cost to bail Madigan outta jail? I'll pay for whatever damages he done too."

"Amanda Sommer will present you with a bill," the samurai assured him. "The sheriff will tell you what bail payment is required when he returns. In keeping with the United States Constitution: 'Excessive bail shall not be required, nor excessive fines imposed,' " he quoted from the eighth amendment by memory. "However, these costs will be rather high since Madigan also assaulted two citizens."

"The dumb bastard was supposed to assault you," Wilkins declared candidly.

"He tried," Tom commented.

"Don't tell me you whupped him with your fists?"

"No," the samurai replied. "I employed other parts of my body as well, but I used no other weapon."

105

"Well, you're a mighty impressive feller, Fletcher," Wilkins stated. "You ain't like no deputy I ever met up with before. Ain't like anybody I can recall. I figure I can put my cards on the table with you. Whatta you say?"

"What do your cards have to do with this matter?" Tom asked, confused by the rancher's expression.

"I mean I'm going to tell you outright what I want and what's gonna happen if I don't get it."

"Tell us both, Wilkins," Hal Newton demanded as he entered the office. He slammed the door hard. "First off you can explain why the hell you sent that big Irish jasper into town to try to pick a fight with Tom."

"Madigan was supposed to put your deputy out of action for a spell," the rancher answered. "Bust an arm or maybe a leg, but nothin' more'n that."

"Witnesses tell me it sure looked like he was tryin' to kill Tom with that broken beer mug," the sheriff snapped.

"Maybe he got desperate when he started to lose the fight," Wilkins shrugged. "Anyway, I told him just to break a bone or two. No maimin', no cripplin' injuries."

"Don't expect us to thank you," Newton hissed. "You're as guilty as Madigan!"

"So I'll pay my own bail while I'm here."

"You didn't want Tom to be able to help me protect my prisoner from you, did you?"

"Don't deny it, Sheriff," Wilkins admitted. "Sort'a figured he might be a bigger problem than you and Jeremy Pike was a while back."

"Takin' one of my prisoners won't be as easy as it was then, Wilkins. I always knew you were a stubborn cuss, but I didn't figure you were arrogant enough to march in here and kidnap a man from one of my cells. Is that what you've got them four fellers outside for? If

106

that's the best you can scare up, I'll put my money on this scatter-gun," he patted the Greener shotgun under his arm. "And Tom Fletcher."

"You listen to me and you listen good," the rancher warned. "A long time ago I trusted a court. You probably didn't know I had a son before we settled here in the New Mexico Territory. Well, I did. His name was Benjamin. He was fifteen when a liquored-up soldier shot and killed him one night in Dodge City. They had a trial and they decided it was an accident," Wilkins's face expressed his rage, although tears formed in his eyes. "They sentenced him to three lousy years in an Army stockade! Three years for killin' my boy!"

The rancher wiped a calloused palm across his moist eyes. "We moved away after that. Left Kansas and headed here to be where a man could still expect some justice because he was able to make it for himself. And now you expect me to allow another judge and jury to let one of the murderers of my wife and daughter go free or spend three damn years in a prison while my kin lay six feet under?" Wilkins shook his head, trembling with rage. "No! Nothin' is gonna stop me from handling this myself!"

The door opened and Clay Young appeared in the entrance with a pistol in his fist. "Heard some yellin' in here," he declared. "You need any help, Mister Wilkins?"

"Get out of here, you jackass!" the rancher snapped. "If I want you, I'll call you. In the meantime, stay out there like I damn well ordered."

"Wilkins," Newton began. "Matt. I'm sorry about what happened. But that doesn't mean every court is gonna go easy on the guilty party when they pass sentence."

"You can't say it won't happen again," Wilkins insisted. "You can't say for certain."

"Don't you think *I* want to see Carlos Alverez punished as much as you do? He killed Jeremy Pike, who was my friend as well as my deputy."

"Friends ain't the same as kin," the rancher declared. "I got me a right to revenge. The Good Book says so."

"Yeah," the sheriff sighed. "That's already been pointed out to me," he glanced at Tom as if the samurai was somehow responsible for Wilkins's Biblical defense. "The fact remains I'm sworn to see to it a prisoner in my custody gets a proper trial. I ain't gonna hand him over to you and you ain't gonna take him. Now you . . ."

"You've said your piece, Sheriff," Wilkins declared. "And I reckon you don't leave me no choice."

"Is that a threat?" Newton demanded.

"Hell, no," the rancher replied as he moved to the door. "That's a *fact!*" He looked at Tom. "You'd better move on, Fletcher. This ain't your town and you got no call to stay."

"Yes, I do," the samurai stated.

"Your decision, feller," Wilkins left the office, banging the door shut.

Newton turned to Tom. "It ain't too late. You can still ride outta here."

"No, I cannot," the samurai replied simply.

"Well, I'm glad for your help but . . ."

"Wilkins did not stay to bail out his man," Tom said suddenly.

"Reckon he forgot all about it after gettin' all worked up."

"Or something else took precedent over his other thoughts," Tanaka Tom announced as he rushed to the cell block.

Carlos Alverez lay stretched out on his bunk, staring at the ceiling and humming softly to himself. Madigan, in the cell next to the bandido stood with his fists clenched around the barred door.

"I heard Mister Wilkins's voice," the Irishman declared, speaking thickly with two split lips and a painfully sore jaw. "Did he come to bail me out?"

The samurai ignored him and gazed into Carlos's cell, his pistol already in his hand. The young bandit stared up at the deputy, fear filling his eyes. Tom thrust the Colt between the bars and thumbed back the hammer.

"No!" Carlos screamed, covering his head with his arms and curling his legs tightly under his rump as if somehow he could make himself bullet-proof.

The .45 roared. The muzzle flash lit up the cell with an orange glare. Metal clanged as it struck the hard adobe floor, the sound lost among the echoing boom of Tom's gunshot. Carlos slowly unfolded his arms, amazed to discover he had not been injured.

"Stay where you are," the samurai ordered.

"*Cristo*," Carlos whispered. "Are you *loco*?"

"No wonder he fights like a madman," Madigan said. "Saints preserve me, he *is* a madman!"

Newton appeared beside his deputy. "Tom, what the hell? . . ."

The samurai gestured with his smoking revolver to indicate the object on the floor of Carlos's cell. A Colt pistol, not unlike Tom's own, lay with its trigger guard smashed by the samurai's bullet. A bloodstained finger jutted from under the gun like a thick, pink worm.

"Someone tried to shoot our prisoner," Tom explained. "I saw the hand with the pistol poke between the bars of the cell window."

"Jesus," the sheriff muttered. "That Matt Wilkins is an impatient sonofabitch!"

Newton had the cell windows thickly covered with adobe to prevent further attempts on Carlos's life or efforts by El Halcón to sneak his brother a weapon. No sooner had the sheriff and Tom finished supervising the patchwork and returned to the office, than knuckles rapped on the door.

"We're popular today," Newton muttered. "Come in!"

Tall, dignified Arnold Dell, the mayor and town banker; Joel Stewart, the cobbler; Burl Davidson, Marzo Viento's nervous barber; the Reverend Baker, and Father Santos squeezed into the office. Dell and Baker appeared righteously determined, but the others wore a sheepish expression as if they felt no pride in their reason for being present.

"Well, quite a little group we got here, ain't it?" the sheriff mused. "What brings all you fellers together for this visit?"

"As a duly elected official," Dell began. "I asked these gentlemen to join me as a citizens' committee to discuss the problems that have blighted Marzo Viento recently."

"I'm listening," Newton assured them.

"All this violence and bloodshed has got to end!" the preacher declared. "Shootings, brawlings, the town filled with bandits ready to tear it apart . . ."

"Skip the list of recent events," Newton snapped. "I know all about what's happened. I live here too, remember?"

"El Halcón and his cutthroats are gonna kill us all if'n you don't give 'im his kid brother," Joel Stewart commented.

"You're sworn to uphold and protect the welfare of this community," Burl Davidson said, nodding his head as if to convince himself of his words. "What's best for all is what you gotta do."

"Sí," Father Santos agreed. "And if the bandidos come and kill everybody, then there is no community."

"Simply put, Sheriff," Dell stated, "we demand that you release Carlos Alverez immediately and allow him to return to his outlaw brother before *everyone* suffers."

110

"Don't you folks care that he killed Jeremy Pike *and* Jeff Colby, the teller from your bank, Arnold?" Newton inquired, but recalling Dell's casual attitude toward Colby's death, he didn't really think that mattered much to the banker-mayor.

" '*Let the dead bury the dead*,' Sheriff," Baker insisted. "Only our Savior could bring the dead back to life. We must think of the living."

"Sí," Santos remarked. "My congregation is already quite small. I can't afford to lose anyone." Several eyes glared at him. "It was a little joke," he shrugged.

"Ain't nobody laughin', *padre*," Joel growled.

"This Carlos Alverez is not worth endangering the lives of everyone in Marzo Viento," Dell declared. "I don't like this any more than you do, Sheriff, but we have to face facts. El Halcón has too many men for us to fight."

"What the hell do any of you yellow bastards know about fighting?" Newton snapped.

"Sheriff! Your language. . . ." the reverend began.

"You people are cryin' a lot about safety and the welfare of the town, but what about justice? Don't that matter to you fine virtuous citizens?"

"The Alverez boy is never going to stand trial," Dell insisted. "If El Halcón doesn't get him back alive and unharmed, that crazy Wilkins will kill him first. If that happens, the bandidos will take it out on the whole town. Where's the justice in that, Hal?"

"Justice has nothing to do with this matter," the reverend told them. "Hanging a man with or without a trial is vengeance, plain and simple. '*Vengeance is mine sayth the Lord*.' You should read your Bible, Sheriff."

"I did, and it sure doesn't support lettin' Carlos go free," Newton sighed. He glanced at Tom. The samurai merely shrugged and continued to clean his *katana*.

"You better listen to these hombres, lawman," Carlos shouted gleefully from his cell. "They're telling you

111

the truth. Let me go and all is forgiven. I even forget about settling my score with that one," he pointed at Tom. "He probably scarred me for life with that round knife he threw into my face, but he saved my life today, so I bear him no grudge."

"I did not save your life," the samurai commented. "I simply did not permit Wilkins to take it."

"I can't understand why you're doing this, Mister Fletcher," Dell declared. "You certainly don't need the money that a deputy job will pay, and what happens to this town isn't your concern."

"You do not understand," Tom nodded. "And nothing I can say will make you understand. Do not trouble yourself with it."

"Perhaps it has something to do with that whore he's been living with," Baker mused. "That's another thing we want to talk to you about, Sheriff. This man's conduct is disgraceful. Burl told me about that incident in the barber shop."

Davidson's face revealed stark terror. "I figure I'd best be goin'. The missus will be wonderin' what happened to me."

"Stay, Burl," Baker ordered. "Do not be afraid of this heathen and his blades of violence. The Sword of the Lord is greater!"

"But the deputy has his in his hand right now," the barber whined. "I don't wanna stay here no ways. Sorry, Mister Fletcher. I didn't mean to tell what happened. It just sort'a slipped out."

"Do not worry," Tom assured him. "The ravings of this priest do not disturb me."

"I am a Methodist minister," Baker snapped.

"I am a priest," Santos commented lamely.

"Your deputy also behaved like a lunatic when three men fired their revolvers in the air last night," the reverend told Newton. "Just this afternoon, I heard he was involved in a brawl in that hussy's den of sin."

112

"That's true," Madigan called out. "I seen it m'self."

"Worst of all, Fletcher's conduct with that woman is an insult to decency and morality. You should have run him out of town as an undesirable element instead of pinning a badge on him, Sheriff!"

"Would you accept that badge if I offered it to you?" Newton inquired.

"Me!" Baker exclaimed. "I am a man of God!"

"Does that mean no?"

"Of course it does!"

"Then you don't have any business tellin' my man how to do his job," the sheriff told the minister. "And Tanaka Tom Fletcher has done his job better than any lawman I know, so you just shut your mouth about him. What this town needs is a few more men with courage and less hypocrites."

"You're trifling with your immortal soul, Sheriff," Baker warned. "You're taking sides with a godless heathen and a heretic harlot against the Almighty!"

"The hell I am," Newton growled. "I'm just takin' sides against *you*, and you ain't the Almighty."

"I am not a godless heathen, Methodist Minister," Tom stated mildly. "I believe in many gods."

Baker was too horrified by the samurai's confession to polytheism to speak. Arnold Dell held up his hand.

"Gentlemen, this conversation is swaying from our original objective," he stated. "We've tried to talk some sense into the sheriff, but he doesn't want to listen. Maybe if he thinks about what we've said, he'll realize that his distorted sense of duty is making him act irrationally."

"My sense of duty is based on my vows as a lawman to uphold the Constitution of the United States and to enforce the laws set up by this territory and this community," Newton told them angrily. "You show me any place in those documents and regulations that says I'm supposed to let a killer stroll out of my jail cell and

113

maybe I'll go along with you. If you can't do that—and you can't—get the hell out of my office!"

"Come election time, Sheriff," Baker sniffled. "There'll be some changes made."

"If there's anybody left to vote," Joe muttered as he shuffled out the door. The others followed. Burl Davidson apologized to Tom once more before he joined the rest of the citizens' committee and gently closed the door.

"Reckon I could use a drink," Newton remarked, opening a desk drawer to remove a bottle of whisky. "You care for one, too?"

"Sure thing, Sheriff," Madigan shouted from his cell.

"Not you, damnit! That goes for Carlos as well. Open your mouth again, you bandido bag of shit, and I'll bust this bottle over your head."

"Yes, please," Tanaka Tom told the sheriff. "A drink would be most pleasant now."

"Well, Tom," Newton began as he poured the liquor into blue tin coffee cups. "What do you think of our situation."

"The town will not help us," the samurai remarked casually. "Two armies, El Halcón's gang and Wilkins's men, are approaching from opposite sides. They come not to fight each other, but to do battle with us," he shrugged. "And we must face them alone."

Eleven

Tanaka Tom Fletcher returned to the Sommer Place Saloon that evening. His mind remained full of conflicting thoughts and emotions. The laws of the United States of America seemed strange after so many years in Japan. Punishment for a crime seemed slow and tedious in the West compared to the swift executions in the culture where he'd spent most of his life. Carlos Alverez had been seen by numerous witnesses, robbing a bank and killing two men in the process, one of them a law enforcement official.

In *Nippon* he would have been killed immediately as soon as a samurai could get within *katana* range. Some *daimyos* with a more vicious sense of justice may have required a slow, painful death for such actions, but none would have taken the time and effort to hold a trial under such circumstances.

Tom recalled an incident of Japanese justice concerning an unruly samurai in the city of Edo. The warrior-knight's name was Sadaki. He had consumed too much sake and stumbled through the streets one night, singing loudly and shouting in a manner unbecoming one of his class. Other samurai, in charge of enforcing law and order at night, discovered Sadaki-*san*. They recognized their fellow samurai and knew him to be a first level *daimyo* in his own right.

Because the man's rank was greater than their own, they did not draw their swords and strike him down. Instead of a short sword, every samurai policemen carried a *jutte*—an iron trunchen with a prong jutting from the blunt blade that allowed one to snare an opponent's weapon. The *jutte* was a variation of the *sai,* a short forked device with a long center blade, used by Okinawans in *karate-te* techniques. Three samurai armed with *juttes* surrounded the intoxicated Sadaki, but even in his drunken state, their opponent remained a skilled swordsman. He killed one policeman before the others subdued him.

The ruling *daimyo* of the city considered Sadaki-*san's* behavior most distasteful and incorrect. The samurai begged that he be allowed to commit *seppuku* to compensate for his disgrace, but his master denied him this privilege. His crime had been unbecoming of a samurai, so he would not enjoy the honor of a samurai's death. Sadaki-*san* was delivered to the torturers. They boiled him alive as one might a lobster. It was a death generally reserved for *ninja* agents and traitors—undignified and without honor.

To the people of *Nippon*—and Tanaka Ichimara Tomi—this punishment seemed just, but to the American mind it would be cruel and barbaric. Yet, Sadaki-*san* had had a trial of sorts. If he had been a low born peasant, this would not have been the case. Carlos had committed a grave offense and he seemed to be of a less than favored social class. Why should he be granted the right of a trial when there was no doubt of his guilt?

Tom considered this matter grimly. He recalled that twice he had been arrested for killing men and both times he was released when his actions were declared to be self-defense. If a foreigner killed someone in Japan, his likelihood of such an understanding verdict would be slim indeed.

Also: The Six-gun Samurai had a price on his head in California for the murder of a police lieutenant named Sean O'Neal. Tom was innocent of this charge. If captured and forced to stand trial, he would be far more apt to be found innocent if an American judge and jury determined his fate rather than the *daimyo* who sentenced Sadaki to his horrible death.

No one is above the law in any civilized society, but perhaps, in America no one was supposed to be *beneath* the law as well. An odd concept, Tom thought. Yet he did not find it unattractive.

El Halcón had also made an impression on the samurai. The bandido's fearless attitude toward death seemed almost to be *bushido* in nature. In his own way, Alverez had tried to make a reasonable agreement with the lawmen for the release of his brother. He had promised never to return to Marzo Viento and Tom believed Fidel Alverez would have kept his word—just as he knew the bandido would continue to seek the freedom of Carlos and the death of the Six-gun Samurai.

An odd man, Tom thought. An honorable warrior in an unhonorable profession. He was similar to the *yakuza* of Japan, thieves who held to a strict code, not unlike *bushido*. The *yakuza* often used their ill-gotten gains to assist peasants and even helped defend poor villages from marauding bandits and *ronin*.

The samurai mentally chided himself for this comparison. From what he'd learned about El Halcón, the man had no compassion for the poor and preyed upon them without mercy. His men were vicious murderers, thieves and rapists. Perhaps the bandit leader retained some shreds of honor, but he had not disciplined his men to behave in a less barbaric manner. Alverez was not to be admired, although he still deserved respect as a man and an enemy.

Perhaps Matt Wilkins disturbed Tom the most. Just as he could not fault El Halcón for his efforts to rescue his brother, he could not disagree with the rancher's desire to avenge his murdered wife and daughter. He had returned to the United States to seek bloody *bushido* justice for the slaughter of his own family. Nothing had changed his desire for this goal. Every day that he spent in Marzo Viento was another day taken from his quest for revenge. No man would stand between the samurai and the men he'd sworn to kill. He could not allow a court to determine their fate. Their lives belonged to Tanaka Tom Fletcher, and one by one, he would take them unless he perished in the process. Did not Matt Wilkins have the same right to his own revenge?

Thoughts of Hal Newton made the Six-gun Samurai smile. The sheriff's devotion to duty and determination to uphold the laws he believed in was truly admirable. Tom considered Newton the most honorable man he had encountered since arriving in the United States. Had he been born in Japan, what a splendid samurai Hal Newton would have been!

Tanaka Tom parted the batwings and entered the saloon. Oscar Brill, once again seated by a table alone with a deck of cards and a bottle of whisky before him, tipped his stovepipe hat in greeting. Joel Stewart, who seemed to spend all his spare time in the tavern, turned his face from Tom, and Burl Davidson waved nervously at the deputy. Bart Finely, the bartender, announced that he'd buy the samurai a drink in thanks for "pounding snot outta that Irish bastard." Clem Porter scurried away from Tom, protectively clutching his broom to his scrawny chest.

The Six-gun Samurai mounted the stairs and headed for Amanda Sommer's room. To his surprise, he discovered the door had been locked. He knocked and a key turned before the door opened.

"Well, look at who's back," Amanda commented sourly, staring up at him with anger in her clear blue eyes. "What do you want?"

"To sleep," the samurai replied with a grin. "Among other things."

"You can sleep and do your other things in room four," she told him, thrusting a key into his hand. "I had all your stuff put in there so you ain't got no reason to bother me again."

"You seem perturbed," Tom stated. "What have I done to offend you?"

"Talk to your *friend* about it," Amanda snapped. "She's waiting for you. Be damned if I will any more!"

Amanda slammed the door hard, and Tom heard the key turn in the lock. He frowned. Women often became upset about things that men do not understand, but he could not think of anything he had done to merit her rejection. When last they'd met, Tom had vanquished Madigan and prevented him from creating more damage within her establishment. Amanda had been quite pleased with him then. Had she discovered that the reason the Irishman had vandalized her saloon was to lure Tom into a fight? Surely she could not hold him responsible for that.

She? Amanda's word penetrated his consciousness. Who was his "friend"? Apparently Amanda referred to another woman, which probably explained her rage. Females are a jealous lot. Yet, Tom knew no other woman in Marzo Viento.

He moved to room number four cautiously. The answer to the puzzle might lie beyond the door, but mysteries sometimes have deadly conclusions. Tom drew his .45 Colt before he turned the knob. The door was not locked. He swung it open, moving swiftly to the side

119

of the doorframe in case a bullet came hurtling in his direction.

"Do not be alarmed, *Señor* Fletcher," a feminine voice urged. "I am not armed."

The samurai entered the room slowly, his senses alert and prepared for an ambush. A woman stood by the framed bed. Dressed in a white blouse with a low neckline, offering an intriguing view of cleavage, and a long multicolored skirt, she appeared to be a Mexican girl in her middle twenties.

"My name is Maria Mendez," she replied. "And I have come to you for help."

Tom tried to dismiss the fact she was very lovely. Her long black hair extended beyond her shoulders and her large dark eyes were expressive and appealing. Maria's mouth was sensuously wide and her dark complexion was free of blemishes or scars. "Why didn't you come to the sheriff's office to speak with me?"

"I wish only to see you, not the sheriff," the girl replied.

"Why?" he asked, crossing the room to examine his equipment in one corner.

"I live three miles from here in a small *casa* with my father. He is a very old man, but he is proud. He refuses to leave his home and move into town. This morning, we saw El Halcón and his murderous bandidos ride from Marzo Viento. They must have been eager to go wherever they were headed, for they did not stop. We would be powerless against them, *Señor*. Only you can help us."

The samurai raised an eyebrow. "How?"

"I have heard that you fight like *el tigre*, that no man can stand against you," she declared. "It is said that you, not the sheriff, forced El Halcón to back down this day. Only you can protect my father and me from the bandidos."

120

"I cannot," Tom told her, watching her expression for the reaction to his reply.

"We have little money, *Señor* . . ." Maria said, looking down at the floor.

"Money does not interest me," the samurai snapped, although he suspected she wasn't about to offer him a financial reward. "Convince your father to come into town. My duty is here and here I shall stay."

"A man must do as his conscience dictates," the girl nodded. "So must a woman."

She unlaced the front of her blouse and pulled it off deftly. Her round breasts were firm and perfectly shaped. Maria fondled one gently, thumbing the erect protuberance.

"My body excites you, no?" she inquired.

"It does," Tom admitted, trying to resist the stirring within his loins. "But it will not alter my decision."

Maria calmly unfastened her skirt. It fell to her feet, revealing her long tapered legs and smooth thighs. She wore no undergarments. Maria lowered a hand to the black triangle and brushed her fingers across the hair slowly.

"I am not experienced in creating pleasure for a man, *Señor*," she declared. "Let me try, however, to bring you pleasure tonight."

The samurai's desire rose within him like the fire of a furnace, yet he knew Maria was being less than truthful. Tom suspected her reason for meeting him to be more than she claimed and he felt certain her remark about being a sexual novice was false.

"I cannot deny my duty. I shall remain here."

"This is not the time for talk," she said seductively. "Come, make love to me."

Tanaka Tom approached her and took the girl into his arms. Their mouths crushed together. His tongue skillfully explored the dark warm cavern. Maria's body

121

trembled with delight. Her hand reached between them and began to unbutton his trousers.

"Standing is not the best way," he whispered.

"We will try as many ways as your endurance permits."

"Then we shall enjoy many variations, if *you* have the sexual stamina."

"We shall see, *Señor*, who tires first."

Maria's legs encircled Tom's, drawing herself closer and driving him into her. A less muscular man may have fallen off balance due to the awkward burden, but Tanaka Tom carried her clinging body to the bed and placed her on the mattress.

Acquiring better leverage, he worked his pelvis steadily, forward and back. The girl moaned in ecstasy, clawing at his shirt in her passion. Tom's motion gradually increased, the tempo of his thrusts corresponding with her squeals of pleasure.

The girl's legs rose, sliding around his hips and locking at the ankles. Tom bent to kiss her breasts and Maria's lips brushed his neck in return. The samurai's artful fingers coasted along the sensitive naked thighs from her rump to the backs of her knees, stimulating nerve centers and pressure points that could produce pleasure as well as pain. Tom's knowledge of anatomy in the study of martial arts, and his vast experience with women had honed his ability as a lover as well as a fighter.

Maria cried out and shuddered in her climax. Tom released her and stepped back to remove his swords and unbuckle his gunbelt. He placed the weapons near the bed while the girl hummed with pleasure.

"It will be better without my clothing," he declared. "Come, undress me."

"Yes, Tom," she responded eagerly. Her hands fumbled at his garments in her haste to strip the samurai.

122

"The art of love-making is best done at a gradual pace," he told her.

"As you say, it will be," Maria agreed.

She removed his shirt, kissing his powerful deltoids and caressing the hard muscles of his chest. Tanaka Tom sat on the edge of the bed while Maria tugged off his boots.

"I have never seen such fine swords," she remarked. "They are not sabers or similar to the weapons used for fencing."

"No," the samurai answered, mentally noting her interest in his weapons and adding it to his reasons for suspicion. "They are from a land on the other side of the world."

"Why do you carry two swords?"

"It is my privilege and duty," Tom answered. "The *katana* and *ho-tachi* were made by a master swordsmith more than two hundred years ago. There is much tradition and honor in my weapons. They are more than steel and sharkskin and twisted silk. The sword is the nucleus of a samurai's being. They are alive with history and love."

"Love?" Mzria was startled. "You associate love with weapons?"

He nodded. "Love and care of many years were devoted to their construction. They are part of a culture that loves beauty and gentleness and recognizes the wonderment of subtlety while understating the grand and impressive. These swords have been in my family for generations. They are the love and the traditions of all Tanakas that ever lived and all that will be in the years to come."

"I have never heard a man speak of his weapons in such a manner," the girl said. "But then, I have never met a man like you."

Maria pulled down his trousers and examined his

123

body with frank admiration. She climbed into the bed on her knees, straddling his loins.

"We have . . ." she began.

"Silence, Maria," Tom whispered. "As you said, now is not the time for talk."

Twelve

The Six-gun Samurai and Maria Mendez enjoyed four hours of magnificent love-making before the girl left his room. She did not mention her father again or ask him to assist her. Tom's suspicion of Maria had reached its zenith, although he did not know what her motives might be.

As he walked his rounds beneath the night sky, Tanaka Tom regretted his sexual excess. The day had been long and difficult and the fight with Madigan, tense confrontation with El Halcón, the meetings with Wilkins and the townsfolk had taken their toll. He should have slept instead of taxing himself further with a woman.

Tom yawned as he strolled by the general store. He shook his head with self-contempt. A foolish action indeed, to tap his physical strength for the temporary pleasures of the union of a man and a woman. He smiled thinly. Maria was certainly no novice. Her skill and stamina as a lover rivaled his own.

The sound of an object cutting through the air ripped the samurai's mind back to the present. Something flashed in front of his face even as his left hand dropped to his holstered Colt and his right moved to the handle of his *katana*.

Strong hemp tighted around his midsection, pinning his arms to his body. He felt the knot of the lariat at the small of his back and cursed under his breath. In Colorado, he had been roped in a similar manner by two bounty hunters named McNee and Niebocker. Tom's body was jerked back into the alley by strong hands pulling the rope forcefully.

Determined not to be captured, the samurai did not resist the rope, but ran backward. The tugging ceased and the rope went slack. Tom whirled to face two startled cowboys, still holding the lariat as if examining a dead serpent. He leaped into the air and punted a booted foot into the closest man's face. The cowhand fell back into his partner and both landed on the ground.

Tom flexed his arms, trying to lessen the rope's embrace. Two powerful arms encircled his chest as other figures materialized from the darkness. The samurai snapped the back of his heel up in a *ushiro-keage-geri*. The man holding him gasped when the karate kick connected with his testicles. He released Tom and wilted to the ground.

A fist smashed into the samurai's face. He staggered and lashed a devastating side kick to the aggressor's midsection. The man fell in a coughing heap, but two others took his place. Tom stamped the bottom of his right foot into the nearest opponent's keneecap. The man doubled with a grunt and Tom's left leg launched a *mae-geri-kekomi* front kick to his mouth.

The other cowboy closed in and threw a punch at Tom's head. Tanaka Tom weaved out of its path and the fist whistled by his ear. The samurai folded a knee and brought it up hard striking a soft abdomen. He recognized the agonized face of Art Moore when the aggressor crumbled to his knees.

126

Tom struggled to free his arms while still more figures charged from the shadows. He dropped another man with a *mawashi geri* roundhouse kick, the ball of his foot crashing into the opponent's ribs with bone-splintering force. A thin-framed cowboy leaped into Tom. They both slammed into the wooden wall of the store.

"We got the bastard now!" Clay Young exclaimed, pushing the samurai's back into the wall. "Help me hold 'im so I can . . ."

Tanaka Tom ducked his head and thrust it upward, driving the top of his skull under Clay's jaw. The ugly teeth clashed together and the cowboy fell on his back. Josh Spencer's fist cracked against the samurai's chin and he went down heavily on his side.

A boot slammed into Tom's midriff followed by a vicious stomp to his hip that would have broken bone had he not been wearing his holstered six-gun. Josh bent and punched the samurai in the side of the head.

"Move, damnit!" Clay Young snarled.

He smiled sadistically and kicked Tom in the face hard, the heel of his boot splitting the samurai's skin at the cheekbone. Tanaka Tom barely felt the next kick to his chest. His mind slumped into the welcome black void of unconsciousness.

Pain lanced through the samurai's skull as his senses slowly returned. The shadows of his forced slumber gradually slipped away. Smoke from burning tobacco assaulted his nostrils. At least his nose hadn't been broken—this time—although he could not be certain about the rest of his anatomy. His body felt as though he had fallen under a stampede of angry cattle, and his head ached as if he had consumed all the sake in Japan and proceeded to drink all the whisky and tequila in New Mexico.

127

"Comin' around, Fletcher?" a gruff voice asked.

Tom's vision cleared and he saw the weather-beaten face of Matt Wilkins less than a foot from his own. The rancher withdrew a cigarette from his mouth with his left hand. The right wore a crude bandage to cover the bloody stump of his right trigger finger.

"Sent eight of my boys to get you, Fletcher," Wilkins declared. "Seems that weren't too many a'tall."

"Hell," Clay Young snorted. "We stomped the shit outta him!"

"Shut up, Clay," the rancher muttered. "Even with his arms tied up he was still almost too much for you!"

The cowboy sniffled.

Wilkins turned to Tom. "Half of my boys were still on the ground when I made what was left stop beatin' on you, Fletcher. A couple of them just come to a minute ago. They probably would'a stomped you to death if'n I hadn't made 'em quit."

"Do you expect me to thank you?" the samurai asked, his jaw smarting.

"Wouldn't ask you to," the rancher stated. "I'm just sayin' I don't begrudge Madigan for gettin' whupped by you earlier today. You're one hell of a man."

Tanaka Tom glanced about to discover he was on the floor of a small room. A rowboat was propped up against a wall with two oars resting alongside it. Fishnets and coils of rope hung from nails, and several crates and barrels cluttered most of the opposite side of the room.

"Where am I?" he asked, testing his sore muscles by sitting up. His arms and legs were not bound, but he winced as the effort rubbed bruises against the floor.

"No broken bones?" Wilkins asked, genuine concern in his voice.

"I think not," Tom replied. "Where am I, please?"

"This is a little shack o' mine by the river that runs

128

through my land," the rancher answered. "Ain't much more than a stream, but in this territory that's a river. Got some good-sized fish in it. Catfish and large mouth bass mostly. You like fish, Fletcher?"

"I often eat fish," the samurai replied, gently touching the gash in his cheek.

"Well, I'd be right proud if'n after this is all over, you and the sheriff will join me sometime and we'll spend the afternoon fishin'. Clean and cook what we catch and have it for supper. With some sourdough bread and a pot of fresh brewed coffee, it'll make quite a meal. Then we might have some good whisky and cigars and sit around the campfire and swap stories," he smiled. "I'd like to hear a few o' your stories, Fletcher. Like to know more about you."

Wilkins sighed. "You see, I don't hold no grudges unless somebody's taken away what's rightfully mine. You and Hal Newton is doing a job and doing what you fellers think is right. Hell, I ain't even mad at you for shootin' off my finger. I was pissed-off like a pissed-on rooster at first, but I figure you was just doin' what you reckoned you had to. Can't begrudge you that 'cause I'm gonna ride back to town and do what I figure I gotta do." He looked at Tom and nodded slowly. "And somehow, I think you understand that, Fletcher."

"The sheriff will not release Carlos Alverez," Tom declared. "He will fight you if you try to take his prisoner by force."

"Well, I purely hope that he don't," the rancher replied. " 'Cause I'm gonna kill that little sonofabitch and there ain't nobody gonna stop me."

"Hal Newton will try."

"I sure hope he don't try too hard," Wilkins commented.

"You would kill him?"

"I don't want to, Fletcher. I could'a had Clay here

put a bullet in you tonight. He's powerful eager to see you dead, but I didn't agree to it. Did you happen to notice none of the boys was packin' irons when they jumped you in the alley? I didn't wann'a take the chance one of 'em would lose his head like Madigan done and try to kill you. Didn't let 'em carry no knives either and when it looked like they might up and stomp you to death, I made 'em stop."

"You will not be able to rope the sheriff in his office," the samurai remarked.

"Now you hear me out," Wilkins insisted. "I brought you here and stayed personal to see if you'd need any doctorin' and to try to explain things to you. Didn't have to do that, so you just listen a spell."

"I am," Tom assured him.

"If'n there's anyway I can avoid hurtin' Hal Newton, I will. If'n he don't leave me no choice, I'll do what I gotta to get my hands on that murderin' Alverez kid. El Halcón killed my kin and I'm gonna kill his brother. Only I'm gonna be a whole lot more merciful than those bandidos were to Connie and little Lisa."

The rancher's face contorted with grief. "They staked out my wife and daughter, naked, spread-eagle on the ground. Then they raped them. Maybe a dozen men or more. Those goddamn scum raped an eleven-year-old girl until they busted her open!" Anger mingled with sorrow, creating a formidable countenance that would have done justice to a samurai fright mask. "Then they worked on Connie and Lisa with their knives. God knows how long it took before they finally died. Those bastards even relieved themselves on the corpses afterward, as if my wife and daughter was nothin' but compost dump. Tell the truth, Fletcher: Would you be willin' to let some other man have your vengeance after somethin' like that happened?"

"No, I wouldn't," Tom admitted with a sigh. "But

130

you must wait for your revenge. No one is denying you justice. Hal Newton believes in justice as much as you or I. For that reason he'll die to uphold the laws he believes in."

"Like I said before, I hope it don't come to that, but I also hope you'll understand if'n it does."

The rancher moved to the cluttered side of the room and gestured toward the *katana, ho-tachi*, Colt .45 and *shurikens* placed on two of the barrels. "I know you hold these swords mighty dear. Don't blame you neither. They're right fine-lookin' weapons," he said. "Don't figure it's a good idea to let you have 'em right now, not the six-gun nor these—whatever you call these other things. Still, I'll leave 'em right here so's you can see they're safe 'n' sound."

"For your consideration, I thank you," the samurai said sincerely.

"I'm also leavin' Clay and Art here to keep an eye on you," the rancher continued. "Now, you know they got cause not to like you much, so if'n you try to escape they'll be right glad to put a bullet in you."

"Perhaps they shall do so whether I attempt to escape or not."

"I told them I do not want you harmed in any way unless it's absolutely necessary. They got instructions to shoot to wound, not to kill if'n it comes to that. 'Course, they ain't as good at marksmanship as you are, so don't count on that if'n you get any ideas. It's gonna cost 'em a month's wages if'n they kill you. I figure that'll discourage Clay and Art from shootin' you unless you force their hand."

"Mister Wilkins!" Clay exclaimed. "What if we gotta shoot this feller in self-defense? You ain't gonna take our pay then, is you?"

"If'n you kill him," the rancher nodded.

"But . . ."

"He ain't armed, Clay," Wilkins snapped. "As good as he is with his hands and feet, he can't beat a bullet. If'n he tries to get his weapons, you put a round in an arm or a leg."

"What if he manages to get a'hold of that six-gun or one o' them swords?" Clay insisted.

"He's deadly fast with that saber, Mister Wilkins," Art Moore added.

"If that happens you two are even bigger idiots than I figure you are!" the rancher replied angrily. "You deserve to be out a month's pay 'cause you'd have to be too stupid to know how to spend it anyway. You've had enough run-ins with Fletcher that you should'a learned not to underestimate him by now. *Don't* let him near his weapons, and *don't* kill him."

"Aw-right, Mister Wilkins," Clay muttered.

"And another thing," their employer announced. "Don't touch them swords of his. He values them highly and you just keep yore hands off'a them."

"Yessir," Clay agreed reluctantly. Art nodded.

"All right," Wilkins declared. "I reckon that's all I gotta say for now. Time for me to go."

Tanaka Tom rose unsteadily from the floor. His midsection and chest felt as though it had slivers of glass imbedded in it. "Mister Wilkins," he croaked.

"I'm listenin', Fletcher," the rancher assured him.

"You are an honorable man and you understand devotion to duty," the samurai began. "I owe Hal Newton my life."

"So I heard," Wilkins nodded. "Figure that's why you became his deputy."

"If you kill him, I shall be obliged to avenge his death," Tom said sternly.

"I appreciate you warnin' me, Fletcher," the rancher replied. "Reckon both of us better hope the sheriff don't force me to kill him. If'n he does, I'll just have to come back here and kill you too."

He adjusted the white Stetson on his head and left the shed. Tanaka Tom silently cursed himself again. It had been foolish to tell the rancher he'd avenge Newton's death. His samurai pride had caused him to make a serious mistake. The arrogance of his aristocratic position in Japan had caused him problems before. He would have to temper his former attitudes in the future—if he lived to see the next sunrise.

The sound of numerous horses hooves penetrated the shack. Clay Young turned up the flame of the single kerosine lantern while Art Moore held his Smith & Wesson in his fist, the muzzle pointed at Tom."

"Check and see if'n the old man has gone yet," Clay ordered, drawing his Colt from its holster to aim it at his captive.

Art opened the door and peered outside. "Somebody's got a lantern so's they don't ride into a gopher hole out there in the dark."

"If'n you can see that then Wilkins and the rest of the boys are still too damn close," Clay growled.

Art hopped back into the shed, an alarmed expression filling his plump face. The samurai's features remained impassive.

"What the hell are you thinkin' on, Clay?" the other cowboy demanded.

"Ain't you had enough of this feller?" Clay snapped. "He's bad-mouthed us, beat us up and damn near killed us."

"But, Clay . . ."

"When I told Old Man Wilkins about Carlos Alverez, I figured he might give me some kind'a reward," Clay said bitterly. "Walt Jennings is gonna retire as foreman in six months, but did Wilkins even suggest you or me might be promoted to replace him? He didn't give us no money or even promise to give us a couple days off from work. Hell, he didn't even thank us. I've always admired Matt Wilkins. He's strong and he's got plenty o' guts, but he don't care how we feel or what's on our minds."

"Clay, you're talkin' crazy!"

"I sort'a thought of Matt Wilkins like a father," Clay confessed. "My own pa died when I was only nine. None of that matters now."

"But we'll lose a month's pay!"

"I don't give a shit no more!"

"Clay, I ain't gonna take part in no murder," Art insisted. "There's a limit to what a feller can do . . ."

"So just shut up!" Clay snapped. "You just shut up and don't interfere," he smiled coldly at the captive. "We're gonna wait until Big Matt and his boys is far enough away not to hear this gun go off and then I'm gonna kill myself a deputy."

Thirteen

Tanaka Tom's expression remained calm. Clay Young's declaration neither frightened or surprised him. The cowboy's hatred for the samurai had been obvious, and his irrational mind had decided that killing Tom would punish Wilkins for his indifference toward Clay. Yet, Clay Young was neither a trained warrior or a born killer. He might not carry out his threat and Art Moore, although willing to indulge in rowdy mischief with his friends, obviously would not participate in murder.

However, whether he lived or died did not concern the Six-gun Samurai as much as the two *bushido*-bound duties that motivated his present existence. If Clay Young killed him, Tom might yet be able to carry out his vengeance on Colonel Hollister in his next incarnation, but Hal Newton needed his help immediately. Honor dictated he attempt to avoid death and hurry to the sheriff's aid.

Clay Young and Art Moore, although not professional gunmen, were armed and Tom was not. To fight any man holding a weapon, especially a gun, with one's bare hands is always hazardous. Two armed men doubled the risk. He glanced about, hoping to find something to use against his captors. The boat oars within arms reach filled him with expectation.

The paddles of the canoe were shaped in a style similar to the *naginata* he'd trained with in Japan. The long shaft and flattened end of each oar could serve in a manner not unlike the Japanese halbred. In fact, Tom recalled, the ingenious martial artists of Okinawa used a boat oar called a *kai* as a weapon after the Japanese government forbid them to possess conventional weapons.

Clay Young's Colt remained aimed at the samurai's chest and the cowboy's attention was riveted on his intended victim. Although distressed, Art Moore still held his Smith & Wesson, his nervous gaze shifting from Tom to Clay. The samurai realized he'd need a distraction before he could make his move.

"Seems there's been just about enough time for Matt Wilkins and the boys to be out of hearin'-range," Clay remarked. "If'n you know any prayers, Deputy, you'd better say 'em now 'cause in a couple 'a minutes I'm gonna squeeze this trigger."

"Come on, Clay," Art insisted. "You're gonna get us both in an awful mess . . ."

"You goin' against me, Art?" the scrawny cowhand demanded.

"No, but . . ."

"You tell Wilkins I killed this jasper and you tried to stop me, but I wouldn't listen. I don't aim to stay around here after tonight no how."

"Listen," Tom urged, raising his head in an alert manner. "Hoofbeats."

The captors frowned. The only sounds outside the shed were the soft ripple of the river and the familiar chorus of crickets and frogs. Yet, Clay and Art strained their ears, and in the natural habit of men, gazed about as though they might be able to see through the surrounding walls to locate something they failed to hear. A slight distraction, but Tom hoped it would be enough.

The samurai seized one of the oars and charged his opponents. He brought the paddle down hard on Art Moore's wrist. If he had wielded an actual *naginata*, the metal blade of the halbred would have chopped off the cowboy's hand. The edge of the maple wood shattered bone on impact. Art cried out and the S&W fell from his numb fingers.

Clay tried to adjust his aim as the swiftly moving samurai closed in. The oar swung in a *yoko-uke* block and the paddle slapped the cowpuncher's Colt-filled hand into the wall. The revolver exploded, blasting a harmless bullet across the room.

Tom pressed the oar hard, pinning Clay's gun hand to the wall. Still exerting pressure with the paddle, the samurai launched a *yoko geri keage* to Art Moore's midsection. The powerful side kick doubled up the chubby cowboy. He fell to all fours and screamed when his broken wrist protested his hand's contact with the floor.

The Six-gun Samurai twisted the shaft of the paddle, grinding it into Clay's captive hand. Fingers popped open and the Colt dropped from his grasp. Clay cursed, but ignored his aching hand and threw a savage kick at Tom's groin.

Gripping the oar in a two-handed hold, the samurai executed a *morote-uke* block. Clay's shin connected painfully with the shaft of the paddle. He staggered back and Tom slashed the oar overhead to bring the wooden blade down on Clay's collarbone. The cowboy whimpered and fell to one knee. Tom stepped forward and kicked him under the jaw, the heel of his boot nearly snapping Clay's neck when his head whipped back in a violent jerk.

Clay crumbled in an unconscious lump and Tom

turned to see the kneeling Art Moore attempt to retrieve the fallen revolver with his unimpaired hand. The samurai swung the oar low and hurled it. The paddle skidded across the floor rapidly, the shaft striking the S&W to sweep it beyond the cowboy's reach.

"Oh, shit," Art groaned. "Not again!"

Tanaka Tom Fletcher picked up his gunbelt from the keg of nails and buckled it around his lean waist. "Get up," he ordered.

Art obeyed. The samurai slid his *katana* and *ho-tachi* into his sash before returning the *shurikens* to their place inside the *obi*. "I don't know how to get to Marzo Viento from this place," he said. "Your partner shall be unconscious for sometime, so you shall guide me."

"Hell, we can't go ridin' around in the dark!" the cowboy exclaimed.

"We shall take this lantern to provide light," Tom instructed. "Clay Young will not have need of his horse for a while, so I shall borrow it."

"Wilkins will probably already have the Alverez kid doin' a jig at the end of a rope," Art muttered.

"Pray he has not harmed Hal Newton, because of this delay or you shall suffer," the samurai told him. "Do you still wish to waste more time?"

"Let's go, Deputy!" Art nodded fearfully.

When Tanaka Tom did not return to the office after the time for relieving his watch arrived, Hal Newton suspected something had happened to his deputy. With his shotgun in his hands, the sheriff stepped outside. He locked the door, wishing there was some way to bolt it as well. Perhaps he should have stayed in the office and barricaded it against a possible attempt by El Halcón or Matt Wilkins to seize Carlos, but his concern for Tom overruled his better judgment.

Fidel Alverez had sworn to kill the samurai and

Wilkins had already tried to put him out of action. Tom had placed himself in an extremely dangerous position because he felt obligated to Newton. The sheriff could not sit in his office and wring his hands with despair when he knew the deputy might be in trouble.

Newton marched along the plankwalk, cautiously peering into each alley before passing. The streets seemed deserted. There was no sign of Tom or evidence that any violence had befallen him. The sheriff didn't see the two cowboys leap down from the roof of the general store behind him.

The assailants pounced on Newton's back and all three men sprawled to the ground in a tangled, kicking heap. Strong hands twisted the Greener from the sheriff's grasp as the other man struggled with the lawman. Although he lacked the samurai's knowledge of karate, Newton had been in enough brawls to acquire a few fighting tactics of his own.

He rammed an elbow into the wrestler's ribs and broke free to grapple with the man holding the scattergun. Newton slammed a fist into the cowboy's face, then seized the Greener with both hands and jerked it up to crack the double barrels against his opponent's jaw.

Other cowboys quickly converged on the sheriff. He drove the butt of his shotgun into one man's gut, but two big cowpunchers grabbed the lawman's arms and Josh Spencer hammered two punches to Newton's belly, then followed-up with a solid right cross to the chin. The sheriff's knees buckled and he hung limply in the grip of the other men.

"He's pretty tough for an old man," Josh remarked, rubbing his knuckles.

Suddenly, the sheriff displayed how tough he really was. His leg rose and drove a boot into Spencer's narrow chest, knocking the bearded cowboy to the ground. Newton jerked his right arm out of one man's grasp and

139

crashed his fist into the nose of the cowhand holding his left. A blow behind the ear dropped the lawman to his knees. Another punch to the back of the skull put him flat on his face.

"That's enough," Matt Wilkins demanded. The rancher walked from an alley and shook his head. "You boys ain't too impressive tonight."

"We got 'im, Mister Wilkins," Josh Spencer declared. He and the other men dragged the stunned sheriff to a nearby hitching rail.

"Just tie him down," the rancher instructed. "No need to hit him any more."

They lashed Newton's wrists to the rail with rawhide straps. Wilkins nodded with satisfaction, pleased that he hadn't been forced to kill the lawman. Newton groaned and raised his aching head.

"Tom," he began thickly. "What did you do to him?"

"Fletcher is alive and he ain't hurt to speak of," the rancher replied. "If he don't try nothin' stupid, he'll stay that way. I explained myself to him, so he'll just have to tell you about it when he gets back. I gotta take care of some unfinished business right now."

"Don't do it, Wilkins!" Newton warned. "You've already broken a bushelful of laws, but I'll forget it if you don't go no further."

"Laws don't interest me much," the rancher said. "Laws ain't justice and that's what I'm gonna have today. Like the Good Book says, 'An eye for an eye.' "

"The law has to apply to everyone or it don't mean nothin'!" the sheriff snarled.

Wilkins ignored him. "You'll probably find the key to the office in the sheriff's pocket, Josh. Time for us to take care of Carlos Alverez."

Hal Newton strained helplessly against the bonds and watched Wilkins and his men move purposefully to the law office. The sheriff glanced about desperately, hoping to find some way to free himself. Faces of the townspeople appeared in windows like fleeting apparitions before their owners pulled down blinds or drew draperies together to hide from the grim drama outside.

"Somebody help me!" Newton cried, his voice expressing anger and frustration. "They're gonna lynch a man, damnit! You've gotta stop them! Get out here, you gutless bastards! Is every goddamn son of a bitch in this town a stinkin' coward?"

Amanda Sommer emerged from the Sommer Place Saloon, but Bart Finely and Joel Stewart grabbed her arms and pulled the protesting woman back into the building. Screams of terror filled the night as Wilkins's men dragged Carlos Alverez from the sheriff's office. The tall figure of Jethro Madigan limped among the other cowboys who followed Matt Wilkins into the street.

"Where do you want the rope, Mister Wilkins?" Johnny Slade, a broad-faced former drover with a walrus mustache, inquired.

"I reckon the livery stable is the best place," the rancher answered.

"No!" Carlos cried. "*Por favor!* Don't do this!"

"Wonder how many times Connie and Lisa said that when you animals took your turns on 'em!" Wilkins snarled. The back of his hand lashed across the youth's bandaged cheek.

A beam with a pulley for hauling up bales of hay, extended from beneath the peak of the livery's roof. Slade removed the rope from his shoulder and checked the stout hangman's noose before cocking his arm to skillfully throw it over the beam. He grunted with satisfaction in accomplishing his task with only the dim light of the moon and stars and a single kerosene lantern.

"Wilkins!" Newton exclaimed.

Carlos struggled in the combined grips of three burly men. Josh Spencer led his roan gelding under the beam while Slade adjusted the noose. The rancher stepped close to the terrified bandido and seized the boy's shirt front. Blood soaked the bandage on Wilkins's maimed hand, but he didn't notice as he glared into Carlos's face.

"Do you remember when you and the rest of the scum in your brother's gang hit my spread? Do you remember how you raped and murdered my wife and daughter?" he demanded. "Answer me, you bastard!"

"No, *Señor*," the youth replied. "I was not there. The others did that bad thing, but not me. It is my brother and the rest you want, not me. I did . . ."

The rancher drew up a big knee and slammed it between Carlos's splayed legs. The boy wheezed painfully and doubled up as much as the restraining hands allowed. Vomit bubbled from his lips onto his shirt."

"You're a liar as well as everything else," Wilkins hissed. "Maybe God will have some mercy on you 'cause you ain't full growed yet, but I reckon a pup-wolf with rabies is as bad as an adult. We're gonna string you up by your neck now. The knot ain't gonna be behind your ear so your neck'll bust either. We ain't gonna just let you strangle either. We'll raise and lower you over and over again so you won't pass out. We're all gonna stand around and laugh while we watch your face change colors—first blue, then red, and finally black."

"Feller's gonna be a regular human rainbow," Slade chuckled.

"We're gonna enjoy watchin' you twist and kick in the air, just like you enjoyed cuttin' up Connie and Lisa," Wilkins continued. "Everybody's gonna see you piss and shit your breeches. How's that appeal to your *machismo*, boy? After you finally die, we'll let you dangle until you rot. The crows'll come down and poke your eyeballs out and peel your lips off. Ol' El Halcón will have himself a real sight to behold once he gets a look at you."

"Everything's ready, Mister Wilkins," Slade announced.

"Get 'im on the back of that hoss, boys," the rancher ordered. "Time for this feller to take a one-way trip to Hell."

The cowboys tied the sobbing youth's hands behind his back. Sheriff Newton vainly tried to rock the hitching post loose, but it was planted too firmly in the ground. Sweat from exertion and exasperation covered him like a bucket of cold water tossed over his body. The sound of glass breaking startled the lawman and drew his attention to the figure standing by the hitching rail.

Clem Porter held the jagged end of a whisky bottle close to examine the smears of liquor with a frown. "It still had some in it too," the town drunk whispered.

He placed the bottle against the rail and rubbed the sharp edges against the rawhide embracing the sheriff's left wrist. Newton saw the lynch mob raise Carlos onto the back of Josh's horse.

"Hurry, Clem!" he urged.

The drunk merely nodded in reply and continued to saw through the lawman's bonds.

Matt Wilkins personally slipped the noose over Carlos's head and tightened it snugly under his chin.

"There," Clem rasped.

Hal Newton jerked his left arm free and the rawhide strands drifted to the ground in segments. He clawed at the cords binding his right wrist while Clem tried to use his bottle to cut through the tough straps from under the rail. Suddenly, they broke away.

"I gotta stop 'im," the sheriff declared.

"Too late," Clem sighed as he watched Matt Wilkins raise his arm high.

In the excitement and tension, no one noticed the sound of galloping hooves drawing closer.

The rancher's palm slapped the rump of the roan

sharply. The animal whinnied and bolted forward. Carlos's feet kicked in the air. The hemp rope tightened and cut into the boy's neck. Wilkins and the others watched while the boy tried to scream, but his throat no longer functioned. A dark stain appeared on the *bandido's* trousers. He'd relieved himself in uncontrollable fear, not death. Josh Spencer made a bet with Johnny Slade that Carlos's eyes would pop out of the sockets before the crows could get to them.

A tall figure on the back of a sorrel emerged from the surrounding darkness, bowling over three of Wilkins's men and startling the rest. A long streak of light hissed through the air above Carlos Alverez's head. The rope beyond the knot parted and the boy fell to the ground in an ungainly heap.

Tanaka Tom Fletcher pulled the reins of the sorrel back and brought the animal to a halt. The blade of his *katana* flashed before he slid the sword back into the scabbard in his *obi*.

Matt Wilkins glared at the samurai. Two of his men drew pistols and aimed them at Tom, but he paid no heed as he boldly dismounted.

"Fletcher," Wilkins's angry voice was covered with ice. "I ought'a kill you for that! We got another rope and we'll string the Alverez wolf-pup up again. Don't get in my way a second time!"

The samurai's laughter stunned all present. "Your sense of vengeance is puny and self-defeating," he declared. "You would kill this insignificant piece of vermin and possibly lose an opportunity to have the satisfaction of revenge upon all your enemies."

Art Moore rode his mount at a slow trot, the sheepish expression on his face highlighted by the lantern he held. "Weren't my fault, Mister Wilkins," he said lamely. "He's got more tricks than the Devil hisself."

"Shut up, Art," the rancher barked. He stared at Tom. "Is that what this is, Fletcher? A trick?"

144

"You speak of revenge and justice," the samurai replied. "I have traveled from a land on the other side of the world in search of these things. A man named Edward Hollister murdered my blood family in Georgia. I have been hunting that man down—and all his followers—to kill them. I am bound by the code of *bushido*, the way of the warrior class of Japan. There I spent most of my life and acquired the fighting skills that you have mentioned with admiration. Are these things not true? Do you believe my story to be a trick, Wilkins?"

"Don't trust him," Josh urged.

"He ain't no liar," the rancher snapped. "You said you came here to find Eddie Mears, right?"

"He was a minor underling of Hollister's," the samurai shrugged. "Like Carlos Alverez. I have killed many of the colonel's men, but I have not ceased my efforts to find them all and kill them until none remains. If you wish to settle for the life of this—" Tom waved a hand contemptuously at the boy sprawled on the ground. "So be it. I want *all* my enemies to suffer. I want to watch them *all* die."

"Tom, are you all right?" Newton inquired as he drew closer. The samurai merely nodded in reply.

"Let me get this straight, Fletcher," Wilkins said. "What you're tryin' to say is if'n I kill Carlos it might prevent me from gettin' El Halcón?"

"Did you not know that El Halcón and his men were in this town only this morning?" Tanaka Tom answered. "Ask anyone, they will tell you this is true. He wants his brother released. Alverez and his bandits will be back for him."

"Do tell," the rancher smiled. "Maybe I'll be here waitin' for him."

"If that is your wish," the samurai replied mildly.

"Why can't I hang Carlos anyway?" Wilkins asked. "His bastard brother will still come."

"Perhaps not," Tom warned. "El Halcón's sense of

145

honor is different from ours. He feels it is his duty to free his brother, but would he feel obliged to avenge the death of such a worthless sibling?" He shook his head. "Death is the ultimate release. The bandido might consider such vengeance a waste of time."

"That don't make no sense," a confused Josh Spencer muttered.

"Maybe not," Wilkins admitted. "But I figure this Fletcher is a good judge of character. He understands me pretty good, and maybe he reads this Alverez right too."

"So, you will put this child back in his cage and await the glory of total vengeance?"

"I still gotta let Carlos stand trial?"

"Yes," the sheriff answered flatly.

"On one condition," the rancher declared. "El Halcón himself dies for sure when he rides into town. I can't wait for no trial for him. I want your word on that."

"You have it," the samurai agreed.

"Tom . . ." Newton began.

"We simply will not arrest the bandit leader," Tanaka Tom remarked. "Then he will not be our prisoner and we will not have to concern ourselves with his Constitutional rights."

"Oh, hell," the sheriff growled. "I shouldn't go along with that, but I will."

"Do not look distressed, Hal," the samurai urged. "Today we stood alone against all odds. Now we have an ally and one of our reasons for concern no longer exists."

"Yeah," Newton sighed. "But El Halcón is that other 'reason for concern' and stoppin' him is gonna take a heap of doin'."

Tom nodded curtly. "Then that is what we shall do."

Fourteen

Fidel Alverez sat at a small mahogany table, debating whether to sacrifice his bishop in the hopes of luring Pepe Ortega into endangering his queen. The candles within his tent cast a soft, tranquil light on the chessboard. El Halcón leaned back in his armchair and raised his glass to his lips.

"More wine, *Don* Fidel?" Pepe inquired.

"Only if you will join me in another glass, old friend," Alverez replied.

The servent nodded and rose from his seat. The bandit chief smiled with contentment. The chess games with his valet in the evenings were one of his greatest pleasures. Chess is the perfect pastime for a warrior, he decided. It was challenging, yet relaxing—a tiny war without stress because human life was not involved. When the game ended, all the chessmen were returned to the board. None of them died in battle or suffered wounds or crippling injuries. The opposing army did not claim its opponent's territory to lord over the surviving conquered people. The rules of war and strategy were always upheld. Enemy pieces were captured, not

147

killed. Deceit, treachery, and brutality had no place in chess.

If only life itself could be governed in such a manner, Alverez thought wistfully.

"*Señor Mayor,* I wish to talk with you," Juan Ruiz's voice declared from outside the tent.

"Enter, Juan," El Halcón replied wearily. He didn't want to discuss the grim business of his bandido trade. Someday, he vowed to be able to enjoy the pleasantries of life to their fullest without concerning himself with raids and plunder. Then the chessboard would be his only field of battle and he'd never again be forced to raise a hand against another human being.

The wiry second in command of the bandit gang parted the canvas flap and stepped inside. Juan admired and respected his superior, although he considered him an odd and somewhat eccentric individual. Yet, the mind of a genius operated far differently than that of a normal man.

To Juan Ruiz, a Mexican bandido who'd been born and raised in dire poverty, anyone who could read or write was a being of amazing talents. El Halcón also spoke three languages—Spanish, English, and French—and fought with greater skill than anyone Juan had ever met.

Alverez had been a field officer in the Bolivian Army. Juan had never told his fellow bandits, but as a child, he had admired the uniforms and the authoritative manner of the *federales*. He had dreamed of joining the army when he grew older. In his fantasies, he rose to the rank of *capitán*. He boldly led his troops into battle across the border to reclaim Texas for Mexico. The *Presidente* himself ordered a parade in Captain Ruiz's honor and presented him with a medal for his valor in front of the palace.

But fate had steered Juan into the life of a bandido.

The soldiers he had once admired were now his enemies and he preyed on *peónes* as desperately poor as he himself had been. Yet, he had been accepted into the private army of Fidel Alverez—a man who had actually achieved a rank higher than Juan ever dared consider even in his imagination. He had been promoted to second in command of El Halcón's para-military organization. The privilege had stunned him. If only he could wear a uniform, he would truly feel like a real *capitán*.

Juan always felt humbled in the presence of his leader. El Halcón was the product of a higher social class and possessed far greater education than the illiterate Mexican. Yet, Alverez had praised Juan and claimed he was an intelligent, resourceful man. Juan felt fiercely loyal to his commander—which, of course, was the true reason El Hacón had given him a trusted position of authority.

"Pepe," Alverez called out. "Pour a glass of wine for Juan."

"Oh, gracias, Señor Mayor," the Mexican said gratefully.

"Tell me why you wish to speak with me," El Halcón inquired, stroking his chin thoughtfully as he stared at the chess set.

Juan watched in amazement as his leader picked up a carved black figures with a pointed head and moved it diagonally across the checkered board to capture a smaller ivory piece. Even the methods of El Halcón's relaxation seemed complex and intellectual to the former *peón.* "The men are wondering how we shall free your brother. Frankly, I am puzzled by this as well."

Pepe Ortega handed Juan a glass of red wine. The Mexican nodded his thanks. Alverez smiled while the servant gave him a fresh glass and resumed his seat.

"You have lost a pawn, Pepe," the bandit chief told the old man.

"Sí," the valet grinned, shifting a piece from the back column of the white army. "And you have lost a bishop."

"A small price for your queen," El Halcón declared.

Juan stared in fascination as Alverez moved a small man on horseback in an L-shaped pattern to claim Pepe's piece. The old man sighed and shrugged with resignation.

"Tell the men that I am currently considering the safest method of dealing with the problem," El Halcón announced. "Efforts are already in progress to accomplish this task."

"Miguel and Rafael are missing from the camp, *Señor Mayor*," Juan commented. "Did you send them on a mission of some kind for this reason?"

"Sí," Alverez confirmed. "I apologize for not telling you earlier. I have had much on my mind."

"I understand," the Mexican nodded. "These men were sent for reconnaissance, no?" he asked, pleased for an opportunity to use military terms.

"Not exactly, Juan," El Halcón answered. "But if all goes well, *Señor* Fletcher will no longer present a problem."

Pepe moved a rook forward to endanger the black queen. Alverez placed her in front of the white king. "Checkmate, my friend," he declared.

Tanaka Tom Fletcher mounted the stairs of the Summer Place Saloon. Even his superbly fit physique and extraordinary stamina had been worn to the level of near exhaustion by all that had occurred within less than twenty-four hours. His body remained sore from the beating he had suffered and fatigue plagued his muscles as he scaled each step slowly and leaned heavily on the handrail.

Moving to room four, the samurai inserted the key and turned it in the lock. The door swung open to reveal the lamp had been lit and Maria Mendez sitting on the bed, waiting for him. Although the girl remained as seductive and desirable as before, Tom was too weary to retain any wish to do anything in a bed except sleep.

"I am glad you returned safely, Tom," she stated. "I was concerned when I heard of the incident in the street. You must have handled it magnificently, my love."

The Six-gun Samurai frowned. Abby Watson Dayton, in the silver mining community of Argento Creek, had called him "my love." Thoughts of Abby and her cantankerous father, Windy Watson, generally lifted his spirits, but Abby had used the term "my love" with deep meaning, while Maria employed it in a seemingly casual manner that Tom resented.

"How did you get into my room?" the samurai demanded, recalling that she had left before he'd locked the door to make his rounds.

"I must confess I did a bad thing," she smiled. "I wanted to see you again, so I picked the lock and entered to wait for you. You are not angry, are you, Tom?"

"Lock-picking is another one of your talents," he smiled without mirth. "You are a beautiful woman, an accomplished lover, and skilled at breaking and entering. Is this not too great an assortment of abilities for a poor peasant girl so concerned about the welfare of her elderly father?"

"What do you mean, Tom?" she asked flatly.

"Your performance was less than convincing from the beginning, but now it has become tiresome and absurd."

"I do not understand. What performance are you talking about?"

"When I met you earlier tonight, I suspected you were working for Matt Wilkins or El Halcón. One of them obviously sent you to try to lure me from the town. If that failed, you were to seduce me and attempt to draw me into more sexual pleasures for your master's purposes."

"These things are not true, my love."

She gasped when Tanaka Tom drew the *ho-tachi* short sword from its scabbard. "Do not call me that again, woman!" he snapped. "You will tempt me to cut your tongue out and you know how easily I surrender to temptation when a lovely woman is involved."

"If that is your wish, *Deputy*," she replied, venom in her voice. The hardness of her gaze robbed her of much of her beauty.

"Since Wilkins is now an ally, you must be working for El Halcón," Tom declared. "What were his plans for me? To lure me to some quiet place for ambush? He disappoints me. He gave me his word he would kill me, not some hired hands and a deceitful whore."

"I am not a whore!" Maria said sharply.

"No!" the samurai agreed. "Prostitution is an honest profession. A man pays for pleasure and he recieves it. It is an honorable trade in Japan. Whore is too kind a title for a female cobra like you."

"I am a soldier, gringo," she hissed. "I use what weapons I have. Since I am a woman, my body and my skills with sex serve as weapons."

"I am weary and angry," he gestured with the naked blade of the *ho-tachi*. "And I am growing impatient. You will tell me where Fidel Alverez is, Maria—if that is truly your name. Otherwise, I shall be forced to destroy one of your 'weapons.' Tell me, do you think you will still be able to use your charms when you are no longer beautiful?"

The samurai hoped the threat would frighten the girl into revealing the information. He had no taste for torture and did not want to inflict it on a woman, even a treacherous one like Maria. Unfortunately, there were no professional tormentors in Marzo Viento, so Tom might have to do the grisly task himself.

"Fidel is camped not far from here," she shrugged. "He has many men, you know. El Halcón succeeded in taking half-wild hill bandits from a dozen poorly organized gangs and turned them into a real fighting force. He trained them like soldiers, taught them battle formations and instructed them how to improve their marksmanship and to use a bayonet. How much good do you think that ridiculous sword would be against a group of his troops thrusting their bayonets at you?"

"Perhaps I shall find out soon," Tom answered coldly. "And do not belittle my samurai weapons or you will suffer greatly."

"You are the one that will suffer," she smiled.

"I want the exact location of Alverez's lair," Tanaka Tom demanded. "Sheriff Newton knows this territory far better than I. You will come with me and tell him everything you know."

"Whatever you command, Deputy," she agreed.

The samurai nodded in curt reply and pulled the door open. The twin muzzles of a sawed-off shotgun in the hands of a grinning bandido gaped at his chest. Maria plunged a hand under the pillow on the bed and produced a .32 caliber Smith & Wesson revolver. Tom heard her cock the hammer.

"Even if you manage to use your sword before Miguel can fire his shotgun, I shall break your back with the bullets of this pistol!" she stated.

"He cannot cut me before I pull thees trigger," the bandit chuckled. "Go ahead, gringo. Try."

Tanaka Tom considered his possibilities of survival. Glancing over his shoulder, he saw that Maria's gun was a small caliber weapon. Perhaps he could kill Miguel with the *ho-tachi* still in his hand, but she would certainly shoot him before he could reach her. The .32 slugs would be more apt to cripple the samurai than kill him. To be paralyzed with an injured spine would be worse than a quick death. The bandidos clearly did not intend to kill him yet, or the shotgun would already have blasted him in half. Perhaps a better opportunity would arise.

He raised his short sword slowly and slid it into its scabbard. Maria rose from the bed and crossed the room.

"Carefully, *my love,*" she sneered. "Step into the corridor and do not try any of your clever tricks."

The samurai obeyed. Since the Sommer Place Saloon was closed for the night, the downstairs remained empty of patrons and the hallway unlit. Another bandido appeared from the darkness and removed Tom's swords and .45 Colt. Tanaka Tom stiffened, angered that the man had dared to touch his sacred weapons, but he did not resist. Any shooting would only serve to attract Amanda Sommer from her room down the hall and result in her death in addition to his own.

"How did you all manage to get in?" the samurai asked.

"Through the back door," Rafael Montoya, the other male bandit replied. "Maria is quite good at making locks yield to her wishes. That distraction you created outside also served our needs very much. *Gracias, Señor.*"

"I still don't understand why you rescued Carlos from the gringo who was about to hang him," Miguel commented.

"It does not matter," Maria snapped. "What is important is the fact that we have *him* now. Deputy Fletcher is our prisoner!"

"And Carlos Alverez remains a prisoner as well," Tom whispered. "This will not change that or force Sheriff Newton to release him."

"Shut your mouth, gringo," Miguel growled. "You have enough problems of your own, do not trouble yourself with ours. El Halcón shall find a way to deal with your sheriff just as he has taken care of you!"

"You wanted to know where Fidel's camp is," Maria purred. "You are most fortunate, because we are going to take you there. As you said, El Halcón promised to kill you himself. I shall enjoy watching you die, you arrogant gringo bastard. I hope it will be very slow and painful indeed."

"It will be," Miguel assured her. "I am quite certain of that."

Fifteen

Regardless of his samurai training and his belief in karma and the continuation of some sort of life after death, even Tanaka Tom Fletcher was not immune to fear. He tasted the coppery-flavor of uncertain terror while he rode with the bandidos beyond the town of Marzo Viento. Death can be delivered in many tormenting ways, and Tom did not know which method Alverez might decide to employ.

He tried to block out worse possible punishments the bandido leader might choose. El Halcón could have his eyes poked out with sharp sticks or castrate him or—worst of all, cut off his fingers. A samurai unable to wield a sword would suffer the most excruciating mental and spiritual agony. He would be unable to commit *seppuku* to cleanse himself of dishonor and terminate his misery. How could a man with no hands take his own life? Perhaps he could find a tall cliff and throw himself to a bone-breaking fall that would kill him on impact. There were other ways, of course, but Tom realized nothing would be gained by dwelling on them.

He told himself to trust his karma. It had led him to Marzo Viento and given him the opportunity to free himself from Matt Wilkins's men. Perhaps it would still assist him in survival. If not, perhaps it would allow him a swift and dignified death. His karma lay in the future and he could do nothing about it, except do what he was able when the time for action arrived.

El Halcón's encampment consisted of a dozen tents, a rope corral containing the bandits' horses and three outhouses built beyond the bivouac area. Two campfires burned in the center of the camp and four armed guards patrolled the area.

Before Tanaka Tom and his captors entered the camp, a number of angry voices erupted within the area. A tall slim figure dressed in black emerged from the largest tent, buckling a gunbelt around his middle. Two terrified bandidos, clad in trousers and longjohns, fled into the center of the bivouac with half a dozen of their comrades in pursuit. All of them stopped when they confronted their steely-eyed leader.

"What is this all about?" he demanded angrily.

"Alberto and Ricardo were caught stealing, *Señor Mayor*," Juan Ruiz explained.

"Indeed?" El Halcón raised an eyebrow. "I assume you mean in a manner that does not serve as part of their occupation."

The frightened men stared nervously at their boss and glanced to their accusers, their eyes pleading for mercy. The hard expressions of their fellow bandidos destroyed their hope for compassionate treatment.

"*Si, Señor Mayor*," Juan nodded. "These men," he gestured toward the other bandidos that had chased Alberto and Ricardo, "discovered them stealing money from saddle bags that do not belong to them."

"Is this true?" Alverez asked the accused men.

"It was an accident, *Señor*," one of the bandits replied lamely. "In the dark, we thought we had our property. . . ."

"Both of you just happen to make the same mistake

at the same time," the leader smiled without amusement. "You are no better at lies than you are at larceny."

"I am sorry the men disturbed you, *Señor Mayor*," Juan apologized. "We can deal with their punishment."

"What have you in mind, Juan?"

"Perhaps we shall put their hands in the campfire so they will never be tempted to use them for evil against their fellow comrades at arms again," the second in command answered.

"And they will not be able to use their weapons when we need them," Alverez declared. "A barracks thief is a very lowly criminal, but we do not want to punish them in a manner that will inhibit their ability to fight or leave them bitter enough to consider traitorous actions. Sometimes one must blunt the sword of justice for the sake of expediency."

"What shall we do then, *Señor Mayor*?"

. "The thieves will be flogged. Ten lashes no more. If they ever commit their crimes again, they will face a firing squad."

"It shall be done," Juan saluted.

One of the thieves, seeing the hatred in his compatriots' eyes, decided they wouldn't be satisfied with ten lashes. Fearful of being whipped to death, he turned and bolted. The other bandits prepared to follow, some aiming pistols at the fleeing figure.

"No," El Halcón commanded, drawing his *bolas* from his belt.

The *bandido* leader skillfully hurled the weapon overhead twice before throwing it at the escaping man. The *bolas* struck the terror-driven outlaw below the knees, the whirling lead-filled balls swiftly winding the strong cord around his shins and calves. His legs bound together, the man's feet were ripped from the ground and he fell heavily on his face.

El Halcón marched to the sprawled figure and raised a booted foot above the stunned man's head. He dragged his heel back hard, raking the sharp spur across the bandit's back, tearing his shirt and slicing a long furrow in his flesh. The victim screamed and El Halcón repeated the procedure three times until the man fainted. Blood stained the shredded back of the thief's shirt.

"He has had enough," Alverez declared. "See that his wounds are treated and do not administer more than ten lashes to the other man, no matter how tempted you may be."

"*Sí, Señor Mayor*," Juan agreed.

The bandidos cheered eagerly and dragged the remaining accused individual beyond the camp limits for punishment. El Halcón unwound the *bolas* from the unconscious man's legs as the samurai and his captors entered the center of the bivouac area.

"Ah! Welcome to my base of operations, Deputy," he greeted. "I'm pleased you could join us, but then I had no doubt that Maria would be able to convince you."

The girl slid down from her saddle and rushed to the side of the bandit chief. He embraced her with one arm and kissed her on the mouth. "It is good to be with you again, Fidel," she said.

"*Sí*, the Hawk has missed his dove," Alverez smiled. "But I commend you on your success. Of course, you have never failed me, my lovely Maria. Where ten men would not succeed, you always do."

Tanaka Tom Fletcher swung down from the back of his mount and glared at Alverez. "You have gone to great effort to have me delivered here alive. I wish to know your plans for me."

"And you shall, *Señor*," El Halcón assured him. "When *I* am prepared to tell you."

"*Mayor*," Miguel announced. "I ask that you allow me to kill this gringo bastard."

"I have already told *Señor* Fletcher I would do that myself," Alverez replied. "Besides, there is no hurry. Did you bring his weapons?"

"*Sí*," Rafael said, carrying Tom's gunbelt and swords to the bandit chief.

The samurai's temper flared as he watched Alverez draw the *katana* from its scabbard, yet he noticed the bandido treated the sword with great respect and appreciation.

"This is a very fine *espada*," El Halcón remarked. "Once, when I was an officer in the Bolivian Army, I had a saber, but it was not of this excellent quality and craftsmanship. *Gracias*, *Señor*. I shall cherish it always."

"To take my sword is to steal my soul," Tom declared. He nearly told Alverez if he intended to keep the *katana* and *ho-tachi* he'd better kill their owner as well, but he restrained his samurai pride from making such a brash statement:

"Why do you carry two swords?" El Halcón inquired. "A blade is for close quarters fighting and you also have a gun. Is it because you come from a place where you did not carry firearms? The short sword is some kind of back-up weapon, no?"

"You are perceptive," Tom nodded.

"I knew you were a foreigner and not just another Anglo, the moment I saw you," Alverez commented. "I am also from another land. It is rare to meet a fellow fighting man from a strange country. Come and join me for a glass of wine and we shall talk."

"*Señor Mayor!*" Miguel said urgently. "Be careful with that one. He is a dangerous man."

"I am aware of that," El Halcón assured him. "But I am also a dangerous hombre. Find Raul Rodriguez and tell him to come to my tent."

The crack of a leather bullwhip slashing air to strike flesh was followed by a cry of agony. The lash and the shrieks mingled with the laughter of the spectators at the flogging. Alverez nodded with satisfaction.

"I see the punishment is being executed with considerable enthusiasm," he turned to Tom. "The wine is waiting for us, *Señor*."

With his Remington revolver aimed at Tanaka Tom, Fidel Alverez ushered him into his tent. The samurai noted with little surprise that the bandido leader's quarters were furnished with more luxury than one might expect to find in a bivouac area. A desk, a chest of drawers, a full-length mirror and a brass bed surrounded the interior of the tent. A case of wine sat in one corner near a small china closet and the table with the chessboard still dominated the center of the "room."

Pepe Ortega looked at Tom with a puzzled expression. Something about the stranger alarmed the old man. He seemed too calm and relaxed in the bandit chief's lair. It was not natural for a man to be so nonchalant in the face of death.

"This is my valet and closest friend, Pepe," Alverez introduced. "This is *Señor* Fletcher, Pepe, of whom I have told you so much. Will you get our guest some wine?"

"*Sí,* Don Fidel," the servant answered.

"Be seated, *Señor*," El Halcón told the samurai.

Tom pulled one of the chairs by the chess table forward and sat. The bandit leader dragged the other chair several feet from the table and sat backwards to lean his arms on the backrest as he pointed the revolver at his prisoner.

"Excuse me, but I think it wise to keep a little distance between you and myself," he explained. "How do you like my little camp, *Señor?* I realize that my men are not quality stock like you and I, but they are the best I have been able to enlist into my . . ." he thought for a moment. "Let's see, I cannot truly call them an army and I dislike the term *bandidos.* You are good with words. I remember that little speech you made in front of the sheriff's office. What do you think I should call my men?"

"Whatever you call them," the samurai replied. "The word will apply to you as well."

Alverez shook his head. "No, *Señor.* I am not like them. That is why they follow me. They know I am a leader. It has always been so has it not? Those of aristocratic birth rule and the lesser subjects serve their function in life according to their class. Any other system is folly, no?"

"Perhaps once I would have agreed with you," Tom answered. "But noble birth does not mean noble conduct. One must live by laws or codes of conduct and proper social behavior. If a man does not live by his codes, regardless of his level of birth, he betrays himself. Those born to a higher class who possess certain authority over others, are bound by honor to uphold certain ideals and principles. If they fail to do so, they are no better than the lowest born criminal."

"Principles, eh?" El Halcón scoffed. "Honor, duty, fine words, but what do you do when those things become meaningless? When the world around you no longer cares about honor or noble birth? When they spit on tradition and the way of life that has always been for a family of quality?"

"Honor does not die because others do not believe in it."

"Is that so, *Señor?*" the bandit leader asked. "Let me tell you about my family. My ancestors were great men of Spanish nobility, yet they gave up their comfortable

162

lives in Europe and supported Simon Bolivar. My grandfather died in 1811 in the war for liberation and my father continued our warrior heritage in the later wars. He was an honored hero and continued our traditional way of life when he retired from the service. We had a great house and much land. You might call it a plantation in this country. Hundreds of *peónes* belonged to my father's house. Our life was good, refined and peaceful. All things were as they should be.

"I became a commissioned officer in the Army. I excelled as an officer, as all my ancestors before me. One day I would retire from the military and live in my father's house to raise my own family and continue the traditions of the Alverez line. Then, one day bandits with their Indian allies attacked my father's house. They killed him and slaughtered many of the *peónes* and servants. Pepe's wife, sons, and daughters were among their victims. When I learned of this, I took my troops into the hills and we hunted down every hill bandit and half-naked savage we could find. We killed every man, woman and child—for they had shown no mercy to my father's household.

"The army said I acted without orders. Several of my men were killed in the raids and the military accused *me* of their deaths. They court-martialed me. An Alverez with a fine history of honorable service and a noble family, and they disgraced it by condemning me for doing my duty to avenge my father's murder.

"My brother Carlos was attending the Chapultepec military academy in Mexico City, which is why he survived the bandit attack. He was only fifteen and full of hopes for the life that had always been part of our birthright. I told him what had happened and that the dreams of continuing our traditions had been crushed. So he and my dear friend Pepe, joined me and we began to make our own life the only way we could."

163

The samurai shook his head. "You became a bandit, like the men who killed your father. What became of your honor? Was your code so fragile it vanished so completely?"

"I am not like them!" El Halcón exclaimed. "What I do is to reclaim what is rightfully mine. The Alverez tradition has been destroyed in Bolivia, but I shall restore it. When I have acquired enough wealth, then I shall build a great *estansia*. We will be returned to our proper glory. If in order to accomplish this task a thousand lesser lives must be sacrificed, then I shall take those lives and answer to God for my actions. Did He not make the Alverez family aristocrats over the *peónes?*"

"Your karma presented a challenge and you responded to it in an incorrect manner. You compounded your wrong by choosing a dishonorable path," the samurai told him. "Do not attempt to blame your God for this or justify your actions as an attempt to carry out His will."

"You are truly a bold man, *Señor,*" El Halcón declared stiffly. "And for a man who speaks so highly of proper social conduct, you are extremely rude to insult me in my own house." Alverez gestured at the tent surrounding them.

"I am your prisoner, not a guest." Tanaka Tom sipped his wine. "Despite this charade. Charades are your entire life, Alverez. You pretend you are a warrior and a gentleman, but you are a barbarian leading fellow barbarians, not into battle, but to slaughter people that have done you no harm. You claim your motives are to restore your family honor, yet your actions have no honor. Your duty is to yourself and your goals are selfish. I have no reason to respect a bandit such as you, so don't expect my manners to be immaculate. Like you, I have contempt for lesser beings, especially when

164

they have worked to turn themselves into vermin on purpose."

El Halcón raised his revolver and thumbed back the hammer, his eyes flaming with outrage. "I thought you and I might have something in common, but I see you do not understand."

"I do understand," the samurai replied. "That is why I offend you."

"I could kill you this very second!"

"If that is my karma, it shall be so," Tom shrugged.

"Karma," the bandit leader smiled thinly as he eased the hammer of his Remington forward. "Where did you learn such strange beliefs? What land do you come from?"

"Talk to the trollop you sent to my bed. She can tell you."

"I am asking you, *Señor*."

"Although I was born in this country, it is true I have spent most of my life in the land Westerners call Japan. I became a samurai, a knight-warrior."

"Ah!" Alverez sighed. "So I was right about you. You are also an aristocrat, despite your strange criticism of my actions. Are you trying to anger me into squeezing this trigger and killing you outright to avoid a prolonged and painful death by torture?"

"Perhaps I am an aristocrat, but I am not like you. A samurai's duty is to serve. He serves his master and the code of *bushido*. He is given authority, but more important—he is given responsibility and duty. This is the way of the samurai."

"So you're a servant, eh?" the bandit chuckled. "Do you hear that, Pepe? He would rather be compared to you than me!"

The old man forced a smile. Their visitor did not amuse him. He remained troubled by Tom's presence and his attitude. Pepe wanted to tell these things to his master, but he could not. It was not his place to advise *Don* Fidel in his business matters.

"Every man is a servant," the Six-gun Samurai declared. "We are born to serve our families and the traditions and cultures of our societies. The samurai serves with his sword, others serve causes and religions by their words and actions. Yet we all serve something or someone. Your valet is more honorable than you, Alverez. He serves you and in his quiet way, upholds the traditions of your family and the culture that you claim are so important to you. You, however, serve only yourself."

"You aren't a warrior," El Halcón growled, offended by Tom's remarks that placed him beneath the level of his own man-servant. "You're a philosopher and your code is weak and stupid."

Insulting his *bushido* beliefs angered the samurai, but he realized a wrathful outburst would only please his tormentor. "You feel my philosophy is not strong, yet you backed down when we first met, not I. You believe I am a weakling? Then why do you sit so far away and aim a pistol at me so fearfully? I have seen your courage, El Halcón. You are very brave with forty men to stand behind you or when a single man lies on his belly with his legs bound together by your throwing cord, but would you dare face me on even terms in a battle to the death? I think not."

"So, you're challenging me to a duel, eh, servant?" the bandido chuckled with amusement. "Your arrogance astounds me, Fletcher."

"Are you afraid?" Tom smiled.

"No, I am not afraid of you, servant!"

"*Don* Fidel," Pepe said urgently. "May I speak?"

"Have you not heard?" Alverez snapped. "You are greater than I. Speak, great servant!"

The old man's face seemed to gain even more age in his sorrow. Fidel had never treated him with disrespect

166

until that moment. Truly, this stranger's influence was most dangerous. "I do not think you should agree to a duel with him."

"Do you doubt my ability to be the victor?" El Halcón shouted.

"No, but I feel this man may be stalling for time or perhaps he has some other trick in mind. Remember, your brother is still a prisoner in the Anglo jail."

"I have not forgotten, Pepe," Alverez assured him. "But a duel will not take long."

"For *you*," Tom laughed. "It will be a *lifetime!*"

"We shall see about that in the morning," El Halcón smiled. "But bear in mind, since you have challenged me, the choice of weapons is *mine!* Your philosophy had better be more impressive in action than it is dribbling from your lips like spittle from a senile old fool!"

Tanaka Tom finished his wine and set the glass on the chessboard. "When the dawn comes," he agreed, rising from his chair. "I am weary. Have someone show me where I may sleep."

"Soon your sleep will be eternal, servant!" the bandit leader snapped.

"That too is karma," the samurai replied.

Sixteen

Maria Mendez entered the tent and attached herself to El Halcón's arm. The bandido leader barely glanced at her, his attention still locked on the Six-gun Samurai. The girl purred and gently ran her fingers along the back of his neck.

"You are tense, Fidel," she said softly. "You have the man you want to dispose of. Kill him now and you will feel much better, no?"

"Our guest—excuse me, *Señor* Fletcher—our *prisoner* has accused me of cowardice and challenged me to a duel," Alverez explained.

"You are not going to accept?" she asked with alarm.

El Halcón rose slowly from his chair, his eyes still on Tanaka Tom. His left arm swung without warning, the back of his hand striking Maria's face hard. The girl cried out and fell.

"Is your opinion of his skill so great or is your faith in mine so small, Maria?" he demanded.

"It is a woman's nature to feel concern for her man, *Don* Fidel," Pepe Ortega said quickly.

"¡Callete!" Alverez snapped. "Your attitude offends me as well, old man!"

"Your friends are trying to save your life," the samurai remarked quietly. "Perhaps you should listen to them."

"It is *your* life that shall be lost with the breaking of dawn," El Halcón snapped. "Miguel! Rafael!"

The two bandits entered the tent so quickly, they had obviously been waiting outside. "Have the tent with the spare ammunition emptied. Then put *Señor* Fletcher in it. Bind his hands behind his back to see to it he causes no mischief," the bandido chief smiled coldly. "I hope you will be able to sleep despite the discomfort, prisoner. If the ropes around your wrists cut off the circulation to your hands, I'm sure you'll accept it as part of this karma of yours."

"Señor Mayor," Miguel began. "May I be the sentry in charge of his tent?"

"Sí," El Halcón agreed. "But only kill him if he tries to escape. I just hope you can handle such a task better than the last one I assigned you."

"Señor?" the puzzled bandit inquired.

"I told you two to bring Raul Rodriguez to my tent and he is not here!"

"Rodriguez is using the latrine," Rafael replied lamely.

"Tell him to wipe his fat ass and get over here!"

"Sí, Señor Mayor," the bandido answered.

As if obeying a stage cue, the obese figure of Raul Rodriguez appeared at the flaps of the tent.

"You wish to see me, *Señor Mayor?*" he asked sheepishly.

"I could live most happily for the rest of my life if I never set eyes on you again, you pig that walks like a man," the irritated bandit leader growled. "But I want you to face the man that caused you to feel such terror

169

you abandoned my brother and left him for the gringos to capture."

"But, you told me I did the right thing to return to the camp and tell you what happened in Marzo Viento. Had I remained I would have been killed or captured. Would this not have left you without knowledge about your brother's whereabouts?"

Some of the surliness in El Halcón's expression faded. He realized that his temper had gotten the better of him and he was ranting at his men. An experienced army officer, Alverez knew this sort of conduct would only result in resentment and disrespect among his troops.

"That is correct, Raul," he nodded. "I thought you might wish to see your demon more closely and come to recognize him as only a man."

"*Sí*," the fat bandit said. "He is only a man."

"Confirm it, Raul," Alverez urged. "Step closer and spit into the gringo's face."

"I . . ." Raul glanced at Tanaka Tom. He trembled under the samurai's frosty gaze. Death seemed to blaze within those dark almond-shaped orbs. "I do not need to do that, *Señor Mayor*. I know that you are right."

"Do it!" the bandit chief ordered. "He dies tomorrow, so you have nothing to fear."

"Very well," the pear-shaped outlaw agreed unhappily.

He moved toward Tom fearfully. The samurai's steely eyes fell to the familiar object thrust in Raul's belt. His *tanto* knife, the only item of his equipment he hadn't recovered from the vanquished bandits in Marzo Viento. Raul nervously worked saliva into his dry mouth and puckered his lips to spit.

"*Haaiiyaa!*" Tom shouted, snapping a *mae-geri-keage* kick to the bandit's crotch. The ball of his foot crashed into the fat man's genitals with the force of a slashing crocodile tail. Raul Rodriguez gasped in agony, crossed his eyes and crumbled to his knees. His straw sombrero slipped from his bowed head to be drenched by the green and brown vomit that spewed from the bandit's mouth.

Rafael and Miguel drew their sidearms, but the samurai stepped back and calmly folded his arms on his chest. El Halcón's thumb eared back the hammer of his Remington. Maria still lay on her side and stared up at the tense scene with expectation, hoping to see the gringo die. Pepe's eyes were filled with fear. Even unarmed, Tanaka Tom worried him.

Alverez eased the hammer of his revolver forward. "Still a tough gringo, eh?" he mused. "We shall see how long you remain that way when the sun rises! Maybe I cut you where you kicked Raul. We see how tough you are then!"

"It is not morning yet," the samurai commented. "And don't expect too much entertainment at my expense. To die with such disappointment will make your passing from this life more difficult."

"He is boring me," El Halcón declared with a casual wave of his hand. "Take him away."

Miguel and Rafael drew close to Tom, pulled his arms behind his back, and tightly bound his wrists with rawhide straps. Then they roughly ushered him from the tent and began shouting orders to the other bandits to empty the munitions "building."

Maria cautiously rose and moved to the bandido leader. "You are no longer angry with your dove, Fidel?"

"No," he smiled weakly. "Rodriguez! Clean up your mess and get out of here! I wish to go to bed."

After all the spare weapons and ammunition had been removed from the small tent at the edge of the camp, Miguel shoved Tanaka Tom inside.

"I would rather kill you myself, you bastard," the

bandit snarled. "But to watch you die tomorrow will be a great enough pleasure, I think."

"Your death will come soon enough," the samurai commented. "Do not be so eager for it."

"Oh, sí," Miguel nodded. "You are a very wise man. That is why you are the prisoner and I am the hombre that will tear your guts out with a bayonet if you try to escape!"

He suddenly drove a fist into Tom's midsection. The samurai's body folded and the bandit seized his hair and jerked Tom's head down. A folded knee rose to connect with the prisoner's jaw. The Six-gun Samurai's back slapped the ground when he fell, his head ringing with pain.

"I wake you in the morning, gringo," Miguel laughed, stepping from the tent.

Tanaka Tom opened and closed his mouth, relieved to discover his jaw had not been broken. *Samurai pride*, he thought with disgust. His habit of verbally treating opponents with contempt would be his death if he didn't learn to buffer such comments.

Stunned, he felt tempted to simply lie on his back and rest, but he realized if he closed his eyes he'd drift into sorely needed sleep. Ignoring the protests of his battered, fatigued body, the samurai sat up and concentrated his *zazen* breath control into his *hara*.

When the internal power of *ki* coursed through his weary limbs, renewing his strength to an adequate degree, Tom slowly rolled onto his back and began sliding his arms down. His body was folded like a sheet of rice paper, his bound wrists straining against his buttocks when the pain in his shoulders pierced his concentration.

Ninja agents had acquired the ability to dislocate their joints in order to escape from such restrictions, but Tom had not learned this technique. He clenched

172

his teeth and pushed harder, aware that the bones in his shoulders might crunch from their cartilage. His arms would be useless and he'd be powerless against the bandidos surrounding him if this occurred.

Finally, his wrists slipped by the backs of his thighs. All four limbs aching from the effort, he folded his knees and inserted his feet beneath his hands. Slowly, he slid the bound wrists onto his shins. He unbent his legs and sighed with relief. He stretched out on his back and placed his hands on his chest.

Time was crucial. Miguel might decide to check on his captive at any moment. The samurai moved his fingers to his waist and dug into the *obi*. Cold metal greeted his touch. Fortunately, the bandits hadn't taken his *shurikens*. He pulled one of the five-pointed weapons from the sash and poked the sharp tines into the cords around his wrists.

He sawed and picked at the rawhide knots, his eyes remaining on the flaps of the tent. If Miguel entered Tom would have no choice of action. He'd have to try to throw the *shuriken* with his hands still bound. He doubted that he could hurl the projectile with much accuracy, but even if he hit the outlaw, he probably would not kill him before the man could cry out for help. Unless the *shuriken* struck Miguel in the throat, he'd alert the entire camp. The chances of making such a successful throw were so slim, Tom didn't consider it a realistic possibility.

Seconds dragged by as if time had slowed to a sloth's pace. Hours seemed to pass before the straps finally surrendered to the pointed metal. At last, Tanaka Tom's hands were free. He slipped the rawhide cords into a pocket and moved his hands behind his back to massage his chafed wrists. The circulation had not been cut off by the bonds. The Six-gun Samurai smiled. As El Halcón had said, it was karma.

With the *shuriken* in his grasp hidden behind his back, Tom waited. The sounds within the camp gradually diminished. The bandits had finished flogging the thief and even the moans of the punished man ceased. The samurai heard the fires crackle and the shifting of Miguel's feet outside the tent, but the rest of the bandit bivouac became silent.

Suddenly the flap of the tent snapped open and Miguel stared inside. He saw Tom sitting quietly, his arms behind his back. The bandido grinned.

"What's the matter, gringo? Can't sleep?"

"I am meditating," the samurai replied. "If I must join my ancestors, I want to appease myself with the gods."

"Gods?" Miguel frowned. "You shouldn't talk that way. There is only one God."

"Do you pray to Jesus?"

"Sí. I am Catholic. Not a good Catholic, but better than a lot of the lying scum back in Santa Cruz."

"Then you also worship the Virgin Mary and numerous saints and you believe in the Holy Spirit?"

"Well, I do not worship them, but I pray to them sometimes."

"You have your saints, I have my gods. Is it so different?"

"I don't have to listen to your blasphemy!" the bandido snapped. "You shut your mouth or I'll come in there and kick your head off!"

He pulled the flaps shut angrily. Tanaka Tom rose and silently crept to the entrance. He peered through the crack between the canvas folds. Miguel's back was to him, the bandido still muttering about the samurai's sacrilege. Tom's arm snaked out and his hand clamped over the man's mouth before he jerked him back into the tent.

Miguel's startled eyes quickly filled with pain when Tanaka Tom thrust the points of the *shuriken* into the bandit's right kidney. His scream was reduced to a muffled groan by the samurai's palm.

"Say your last prayer to whatever you worship," Tom whispered. Then he tore out Miguel's throat with the sharp tines.

He lowered the dead man to the ground and returned to the entrance. A sentry walked to the campfire and poured himself a cup of coffee, but he didn't notice that Miguel no longer stood guard by the tent. Yet, he would surely see Tom if he tried to escape.

The samurai moved to the rear of the tent and carefully sliced a peephole in the canvas with his bloodied *shuriken*. He saw the back of another sentry walking around the perimeter of the camp. Slowly, to avoid the betraying sound of ripping canvas, Tom enlarged the rent in the cloth and slipped outside.

Walking to the trio of outhouses, the sentry opened a door and stepped inside. He mumbled to himself about El Halcón's stupid concern for camp security. That moron Juan Ruiz had assigned him guard duty again that night. The silly bastard was as bad as Alverez when it came to playing soldier. He unbuttoned his trousers and thought of the good old days when a bandido's life was full of raids, fine tequila and women. They'd never had guard duty and bayonet practice or drills for horsemanship back then, and they'd done damn well too.

He shrugged down his trousers and drawers and sat on the wooden stool. His teeth clenched when a splinter bit into his backside. Outhouses! More military nonsense. El Halcón claimed it was unsanitary to just go shit in the bushes and leave it. He wanted his men to dig latrine ditches and build little houses over them to keep the smell from bothering his sensitive nose. Why don't the goddamn horses have to uses little houses? Is horse dung more pleasant to smell than a man's? Animals crap where they please and they don't seem to get sick as often as people do.

The door burst open and a tall figure blotted out the night sky. Before the startled bandido could cry out in alarm or reach for his weapon, the rock hard edge of a hand slashed into his temple. The man's head seemed to explode and he slumped unconscious on the seat. Tanaka Tom ripped open his jugular vein with the *shuriken* before he stepped outside and closed the door.

The samurai recalled that he'd seen four armed guards patroling the area. He silently continued to stalk the remaining three. One romantically inclined bandit had leaned his rifle against a tree stump to gaze up at the sky and attempt to count the stars. He puzzled over what number follows *diez* and shook his head with dismay, certain there were too many tiny lights in the sky for him to count them that night. He was right. A strong arm slid around his throat from behind and another slipped under his armpit to place a palm at the back of his skull. His feet were kicked out from under him and his swaying body weight caused the forearm vice around his neck to serve as a hangman's noose. Vertebra crunched—the last sound he would ever hear before plunging into Death.

Tanaka Tom located the third sentry and waited for him behind the cover of a barracks tent. The man passed the lurking samurai and didn't realize he was in danger until two powerful hands seized his rifle. He tried to struggle, but the ambusher was too strong and he'd thrown the guard off-balance with a stomp to the back of the knee. He tried to call out, but the speed of the attack prevented him. One second he had the rifle in his grasp, the next it was across his throat, cutting off his breath. A bent knee slammed into his kidney and the rifle jerked back hard. The man's windpipe crumbled like a dry leaf and he slumped to the ground and died.

After completing his coffee break, the fourth and last

bandit on guard duty turned from the campfire and returned to his task. However, something seemed wrong. The camp was more quiet than usual at night. A chorus of snores echoed from the surrounding tents, but he didn't hear the shuffling footsteps of his fellow sentries. He glanced about nervously. The guard didn't see them either. He wondered if he should call for help. If the others were merely relieving themselves in the bushes, he'd appear foolish to the rest of the gang. His *machismo* recoiled from the thought of being labeled an old woman by his peers.

The Six-gun Samurai solved the man's problem and terminated all his earthly cares with a single stroke of the rifle he'd taken from the last man he'd killed. The steel butt plate stamped into the seventh vertebra at the base of the sentry's neck. Bone cracked and the bandido fell on his face, already dead. Tom kicked him over on his back and plunged the bayonet into his heart before he left the guard.

Tanaka Tom Fletcher crept to El Halcón's tent. Honor demanded that the samurai reclaim his swords and he could also end the bandidos' threat to Marzo Viento by simply killing Fidel Alverez while he slept. His debt to Sheriff Newton would be paid and he could deliver El Halcón's severed head to Matt Wilkins as well. Then all would be well and the Six-gun Samurai could continue his search for Hollister and the other members of the 251st Ohio.

Tom slowly eased back the flap of the tent, holding the rifle with its bayonet ready for action. He immediately located El Halcón. The bandit chief lay in his brass bed, Maria Mendez beside him, her bare breasts resting against his ribcage. The samurai entered and gently walked on the balls of his feet to the corner where his *katana* and *ho-tachi* rested by the chest of drawers.

He put down the rifle and picked up his long sword, raising it to his forehead and bowing in a brief prayer of thanks that he and his sacred weapon had once more been reunited. Tom slid the *katana* into his *obi* and repeated the ritual with his short sword. The samurai then located his Colt .45 and gunbelt and buckled it around his waist. Fully armed, he ignored the confiscated rifle and moved to the sleeping couple.

Slowly, he unsheathed the *katana*, the blade reflecting even the all-but nonexistent light within the tent. Tom's eyes had adjusted to the dark and he was certain he could easily dispatch both El Halcón and his mistress. The samurai regretted the necessity of killing the bandit while he lay helpless. Tom had challenged the man to a duel and he felt obliged to give Alverez an opportunity to face him on the field of honor. However, El Halcón did not deserve special consideration since he'd taken Tom's weapons and insulted his samurai traditions. Alverez would recieve an honorable, quick death by decapitation. Although Maria did not merit it, she would die in the same manner.

Tanaka Tom raised the sword overhead, the rustling of his clothing sounding like thunder in his ears, yet El Halcón and the girl did not stir. His wrists bent in preparation for the first sword stroke. The left foot was poised behind the right. His entire body would execute the blow in the smooth, flawless manner acquired by twenty years of swordsmanship in the deadly art of *kenjutsu*.

Suddenly, the flap of the tent flew back. The shadow of a figure flashed across the would-be victims, the light of the moon creating a distorted inhuman silhouette.

"*Don* Fidel," Pepe Ortega began. "The prisoner has . . ." The old man's eyes met the cold gaze of the Six-gun Samurai. "¡*Ayudannos!*" he cried. "Help!"

178

Seventeen

El Halcón's eyes snapped open to see Tanaka Tom Fletcher with the sword poised overhead. He rolled rapidly from the bed and Maria Mendez awoke with a start to see the flash of the descending blade. Pepe Ortega rushed forward to assist his master, but the bandido had already avoided the samurai's *katana* by scant inches.

Maria was not as fortunate.

The incredibly sharp edge of the flawless steel struck her upturned face. It sliced through her forehead and the bridge of her nose before she could scream. Maria fell back onto the mattress, her lovely features contorted into a mask of horror, divided by the hideous red slash between her lifeless eyes.

Alverez landed naked on the ground beside the bed as Tom raised the *katana*. The bandit leader's bare feet kicked into the samurai's midriff, shoving him backward. Tanaka Tom staggered and nearly collided with Pepe. El Halcón rose to his knees and dove a hand under the pillow to draw his Remington revolver. The valet tried to seize Tom's arms as Alverez cocked the hammer of his weapon.

The report of the Remington boomed within the tent, the muzzle flash dissolved the darkness to display the samurai's stern, impassive expression and the agonized face of Pepe Ortega an instant before the force of the 215 grain lead projectile in his chest hurtled the old man unceremoniously into the returning shadows.

Tom's sword whirled, slashing through canvas as though it were air. He vanished through the gap. El Halcón fired his revolver, blasting two more rounds into the tent near the samurai's impromptu exit, hoping to hit his opponent.

Alarmed voices filled the camp. Bandits were jerked from their slumber by the gunshots and spilled from the tents, weapons in hand, their hearts racing with the excitement and fear of confrontation with an unknown enemy. Juan Ruiz rushed to his commander's tent.

"¡*Señor Mayor!*" he exclaimed. "What has happened?"

He stared into the open mouth of the tent to find El Halcón kneeling on the ground. Tears crept down the bandit leader's cheeks as he cradled Pepe Ortega's head in his arms.

"Forgive me," he whispered, staring into the old man's dead face. "Oh, my great and true friend, forgive me."

"*¿Mayor?*" Juan said awkwardly, unable to deal with the scene before him. The brilliant El Halcón, a former major in the Bolivian Army and the ruthless commander of the most bloodthirsty gang in the Southwest, was on his knees, naked and weeping uncontrollably.

"My last words to him were harsh," Alverez's voice croaked. "It should not have been this way."

Rafael Montoya appeared at the entrance of the tent. "*Señor Mayor*, the sentries are dead and Miguel's body lies in the prisoner's tent. The gringo has escaped."

"Damn you, Fletcher!" the furious bandit leader cried. "Whenever I have something good and decent, must fate always take it from me?"

"Find the prisoner and kill him," Juan ordered.

"No!" Alverez snapped. "I want him alive! He shall suffer such torment before he dies, he will welcome the Gates of Hell! Bring him to me!"

"Sí, Señor Mayor," Juan replied.

The underlings left their commander alone with his grief—and the lifeless shells of his mistress and his only friend in the world. El Halcón rose to his feet slowly, trembling with anger and sorrow. The last of the Alverez legacy was gone and Tanaka Tom Fletcher had taken it from him. The bandit wiped his eyes with the back of his hand. He was still El Halcón and he had the most vicious, best trained bandidos of all time under his command. The town of Marzo Viento would feel his wrath. He would destroy the community and everyone in it. Most of all, the Six-gun Samurai would die painfully for his actions.

The bandits scrambled in all directions, moving in pairs or larger groups. Some saddled and mounted their horses while others investigated the surrounding area with bayonets fixed to their rifles. Hooves hammered the ground as members of the gang galloped from the camp in search of their deadly quarry.

Two men rode to a cluster of boulders less than a mile from the camp. They cautiously steered their horses along a narrow path between the rock formations, glancing from side to side, leery of the possibility of an ambush. They rode single file, pistols in their fists, thumbs resting on the hammers.

Umberto Sanchez's back straightened with alarm when he heard something slice through the air, followed by a sound similar to a machete chopping a melon. He turned to see his partner, still on horseback behind him.

181

Blood bubbled from the stump of the man's neck, dyeing his shirt bright red. The headless corpse toppled from its saddle and Umberto saw the tall figure with the long sword standing among the boulders behind the victim.

The bandido swung his revolver at the samurai, cocking the hammer as he aimed. Tanaka Tom held the *katana* in his right hand and snapped his left down from his ear, releasing a *shuriken*. Umberto saw the blur of the star-shaped object streaking toward him. He tried to dodge the projectile and failed to fully cock his gun—self-preservation taking priority over killing the samurai. The *shuriken* slammed into his forehead, the sharp tines biting into bone to pierce his brain. Umberto Sanchez died in the twinkling of an eye and fell from his horse, the unfired Colt still in his hand.

Tanaka Tom Fletcher shook the blood from his *katana* and climbed down from the boulders. He pried the throwing star from the dead bandido's forehead and replaced it in his *obi*. The samurai climbed onto the back of Umberto's horse, satisfied that his karma had looked upon him with favor. The dawn's light would soon assist him on his journey back to Marzo Viento, and he felt confident he could escape the other bandits who were certainly tracking him. Of course, when the gang failed to find him, they would attack the town, but Tom would deal with that when the time came.

The citizens of Marzo Viento huddled around the sheriff's office. Hal Newton told them what had happened to Tanaka Tom only a few hours before and warned that El Halcón's gang would probably assault the town within the next twenty-four hours. The sheriff had correctly anticipated their reaction. Pale faces stared at him with fear-glazed eyes. The crowd chattered like caged monkeys in the manner of frightened people—who in a group must cope with their collective fear as well as their individual terrors.

"Oh, God," Burl Davidson muttered. "We're as good as dead right now! Oh, God help us!"

"We warned you about keeping Carlos Alverez in your jail," the reverend Baker declared. "Now, see what a tragic crop your evil seeds have produced!"

"Well, Sheriff?" the beefy wife of Joel Stewart snapped. "Why don't you release Carlos right now? Do it this very minute before those awful bandits strike!"

"Too late for that, Mabel," Oscar Brill commented, lighting a cigar stump. "After what Tanaka done last night, I suspect ol' Alverez ain't gonna be happy with nothin' less than a real bloodbath."

"It's all that stranger's fault!" Mabel Stewart declared. "This was a nice peaceful place until *he* rode into town!"

"He didn't ride in," the mortician stated. "He walked. I seen him—and the trouble started when those five fellers robbed our bank and killed Jeremy Pike. Seems to me all you folks were real happy to have Tanaka around then," he glanced at the preacher. "Most of you anyway."

"Sheriff," Baker began. "I warned you about that heathen butcher from the start. He's a tool of the *Devil* just as surely as El Halcón himself!"

Newton ignored Baker's remark, but he looked at Brill with interest, surprised by the undertaker's defense of Tom. "Why don't we quarrel about whose fault this is later? Right now we have to form a plan of action."

"Why don't we leave?" Father Santos suggested. "We could take what possessions we hold most dear and flee the town. El Halcón will surely destroy the buildings, but we will still be alive to build again."

"And where will we run to, *Padre*?" Bart Finely, the bartender, inquired. "We couldn't get far enough away

183

fast enough that those bandits wouldn't be able to track us down."

"We can't run away from El Halcón and rebuild, that's for sure," Jacob Fritter, the blacksmith mused. "If we do that, the bandidos will just come back later."

"We have to fight him," Newton told them. "There is no other way."

"Yes, there is!" Mable Stewart announced. "Let Alverez have his brother *and* give him your sword-swingin' deputy as well! That's what he really wants."

"Mabel," the sheriff hissed. "I'm gonna pretend I never heard that, 'cause I'm tempted to forget you're a female and punch you in the mouth."

"Anybody feel in a sportin' mood?" Brill asked. "I'm bettin' Mabel is gonna drive Joel into becomin' the new town drunk of Marzo Viento. He's probably over at the saloon right now, lowerin' Amanda's stock. By the way, where's Clem got to? Haven't seen him all day."

"Who cares about that disgraceful alcoholic?" the reverend Baker commented with disgust.

"I always figured God cared about everyone," Amanda Sommer said flatly. "Hal, is Tom all right?"

"Just bruised up a bit," Newton answered. "He's bone tired though and restin' up in the back. Hope all this belly-achin' from most of you folks ain't keepin' him awake."

"Perhaps we could satisfy the bandits if we gave El Halcón his brother and sent Fletcher away," Arnold Dell suggested. "They might spare the town then."

"You just put that idea outta your head, Mister Mayor," a harsh voice demanded. "Ain't nobody gonna turn that little bastard over to his gang *or* drive Fletcher outta town!"

The crowd turned to see Matt Wilkins and fourteen of his cowhands mounted on horseback. They also noticed a gaunt figure on a piebald gelding. Clad in clean clothing, two sizes too large for his scrawny frame,

Clem Porter no longer resembled the town drunk who'd groveled for drinks two days earlier. He had recently shaved and bathed and the expression on his face was alert and determined. Clem wore a gunbelt loosely around his waist with a Colt .45 on his hip. No one had ever seen him carry a gun before.

"Thanks for lettin' me use your horse, Sheriff," he said. "Like you can see, Matt and his boys wanted to join the party."

"You sent Clem to get Mister Wilkins?" Burl Davidson asked, stunned by the transformation in the man even the timid barber had treated with utter scorn.

"No," the sheriff grinned. "Clem volunteered to go to Matt's ranch and tell him we're expectin' El Halcón. I just let him have my horse for a while."

"He also give me these clothes and this six-gun," Clem told the crowd. "So don't get worried that I've taken up stealin' just cause I've given up drinkin'."

"*You* quit the bottle?" Bart Finely asked in amazement.

"That's right," Clem smiled. "Reckon you'll just have to clean up your own saloon from now on."

"I didn't come here to have no social meetin'," the rancher declared. "Where's Fletcher? He's the feller that ought'a be in charge of this. No offense to you, Hal, but I figure he's the best man for the job."

"No offense taken," the sheriff confirmed.

"I am here," the familiar voice of the Six-gun Samurai announced. He stood at the threshold of the sheriff's office and gazed at the crowd with an indifferent expression. "I have been awake long enough to hear your comments."

He stepped onto the plankwalk. Tom's face hardened and many of the citizens looked away from him. "I know you are frightened. Some of you wish to flee. Run if you wish, but it will not end the source of your fear.

185

Others feel Carlos should be returned to El Halcón or that I should be offered as a sacrifice to appease Alverez. That is not the way to deal with evil. You do not reward a man for doing wrong. There is only one thing you can do and that is fight."

"That's what we come for, Fletcher!" Wilkins declared. His men cheered in approval, except Clay Young whose jaw had been wired together. Tom noted the cowboy's attendance. Clay hadn't abandoned the rancher, perhaps because now Wilkins needed help.

"You're in charge, Tom," Newton said. "From this minute until the battle is over, this town belongs to you."

"See here, Sheriff," Dell complained. "Giving the stranger command over all the citizens of Marzo Viento . . ."

"Is the only sane thing to do," Brill interrupted. "Go ahead, Tanaka. Tell us what you want."

"El Halcón will divide his men to attack the town from all directions," the samurai explained. "We'll need our best riflemen stationed high among the windows of the tallest buildings."

"That'd be my boys," Wilkins remarked. "I'm still gettin' used to handlin' a gun with my left hand since I sort'a misplaced my trigger finger, so I reckon you'll have to find another spot for me."

"I have a couple'a extra shotguns in the office," the sheriff said. "Tom, do you figure it'd be a good notion to put some fellers with scatter-guns coverin' the street? Nothin' beats buckshot at close range."

"Yes," the samurai smiled. "Your idea is most sound."

"Sure appreciate it if you'd loan me one of them scatter-guns, Hal," the rancher stated, swinging down from his mount.

"I'd like one too, Sheriff," Clem Porter announced. "It's been a while since I used a shootin' iron and I'd be

186

more apt to hit what I'm aimin' at if I use buckshot instead of bullets."

"I got me a shotgun too," Brill grinned. "Business is sure gonna pick up today!"

"Every building will have armed defenders stationed within it," the samurai began.

"Not the church!" Baker exclaimed. "I won't stand for you turnin' a House of God into an armed fortress!"

"You have no choice," Tom told him. "Anyone who is unwilling to fight had best find himself a hiding place and stay there. Do it now, for the sight of cowards offends me and they are not worthy of the company of the brave men who are about to risk their lives for this town."

"I got just the place for you, Reverend," Newton stated. "Right inside'a one of my jail cells."

"You can't do that!" Mabel Stewart cried. "He's a man of the cloth!"

"Shut up or you'll join him, Mabel."

Baker howled indignantly as the sheriff ushered him into the jailhouse. Disgruntled mutters mingled with subdued chuckles. Tom silenced the crowd with the wave of an arm.

"Some of you will be assigned to defend the outside of the town," he explained. "The rest will be defending the inside area facing the street. Women and children that do not take part in the fighting will help the men reload their weapons. This is an advantage we have that the bandits do not. We will be able to load guns faster than our opponents. We also have solid cover for protection, while El Halcón's men will be exposed in the open."

"That's the good news, Tanaka," Brill mused. "Let's hear the bad. If you're gonna fight an enemy, it helps to know his strengths as well as his weaknesses."

Tom nodded. "Thanks to Mister Wilkins, we now

187

outnumber the bandits, but they are still better trained in the art of war and better organized than our people. They are familiar with violence and most of you are not."

"That sure seems to cancel out our advantages," Burl Davidson moaned hopelessly.

"Not at all," the samurai insisted. "The bandidos are no doubt better horsemen than most of you, but you will not be fighting them on mounts. I believe they have suffered few losses in recent times, but last night I killed half a dozen of their men. They now know they are not invincible and this may make them nervous when they ride into battle. On the other hand, they regard this town with contempt and may not think you'll fight. They are wolves attacking sheep and they do not expect us to cast off our wool and become tigers."

"Ain't too many tigers in this crowd," Wilkins commented sourly.

"There are a few," Tom replied. "Even the biggest wolf pack is no match for a handful of tigers. As for those of you that remain sheep, I suggest you grow claws rapidly. We have little time." He turned to Burl Davidson. "Barber, prepare my bath immediately."

"You . . . you wanna take a bath *now?*" the startled Burl asked in amazement.

The samurai nodded. "I must prepare myself for battle."

Tanaka Tom Fletcher ordered the barber to leave him to bathe in private. He washed himself quickly, but thoroughly. To a samurai, the way of the warrior was a sacred duty. There is purity in combat. All subtlety is removed, guile is laid aside and man confronts man in an honest battle to the death.

The samurai dried his naked body and donned a fresh clean loin cloth. Then he opened the parfleche on the table and began to remove his armor. He hummed to himself gently in a subdued chant to the gods, asking that his ancestors look upon him with favor. Slowly, almost lovingly, he dressed in the traditional battle garb of the samurai. At last he was ready for battle.

The citizens of Marzo Viento stared in utter astonishment at the incredible figure that stepped onto the plankwalk. The wide *tsuru bashiri* wooden plate covered his torso, while the *tsubo no ita* portion protected his ribs. The thickly woven *kusazuri* hem extended to his knees and *sode* shoulder plates jutted from his arms like shingles. The *kabuto* helmet with its wide *shikoro* neck protector and hornlike *maedate* frontal ornaments, encased his head and the fierce fright mask robbed his appearance of all humanity.

He wore his six-gun on his left hip and an ornate *obi* sash with his two swords thrust into place, as well as a crescent-shaped knife attached to one end of a length of chain and an iron ball at the other, wrapped around his waist. It seemed as if a man—strange and unlike his fellow men, but still a man—had stepped into Burl's barber shop and a demon had emerged. A demon of war.

"Deputy?" Davidson asked numbly. "Is that you?"

"Who the hell else would it be, you jackass?" Wilkins snapped.

Tanaka Tom raised an arm for silence. The onlookers obeyed. Soon they also heard the approaching thunder of dozens of riders. The sound seemed to engulf the town from all sides, growing louder and more intense as if the galloping hooves could in themselves shake Marzo Viento apart.

El Halcón was coming.

Eighteen

Fidel Alverez's eyes glowed like hot flint chips. Marzo Viento was about to feel the full force of his vengeance. Even his brother's life seemed unimportant now. Tanaka Tom Fletcher had killed the two people closest to El Halcón—closer than his own kin—and he had to pay for that with his life. The entire town had to pay for the destruction of Alverez's dreams of reclaimed glory.

The bandido leader and his thirty-seven men had surrounded the town and prepared to attack. Juan Ruiz commanded half the bandit gang and El Halcón led the others. They closed in on both sides of Marzo Viento in two great horseshoe-shaped formations to encircle the buildings and people of the community. Alverez gave the order to charge. The bandidos in his section whooped with bloodthirsty glee. Juan didn't bother to repeat El Halcón's command to his men. They knew what to do. Pistols fired and outlaws slung rifles from their shoulders as they closed in on all sides.

The defenders within the town had also received an order from their commander, the Six-gun Samurai. They were to hold their fire until they were certain the enemy was within range and they had a clear target. The riflemen stationed at the upstairs windows of various buildings consisted of Matt Wilkins's men. They were better marksmen than the townsfolk and far better disciplined. The reports of their rifles mingled with the cries of a dozen of El Halcón's men. Riders toppled from their saddles, propelled by well-placed bullets that crashed into their bodies.

Unaccustomed to fighting opponents that fought back, some of the bandits abandoned their headlong charge and altered their route to circle around the town. Others pulled back the reins of their mounts and tried to fire into the windows at the snipers above. Five gang members were still blasting lead at their unseen assailants when a lone figure on horseback galloped toward them on a big Morgan stallion.

The man's appearance stunned the bandidos. They weren't even certain if it was *human*. The horseman seemed covered with scales like a manlike armadillo, and it sported two Satanic horns above a hideous face frozen in an expression of pure fury. One bandit aimed a Henry carbine at the apparition, but the samurai's pistol fired before the man could pull the trigger. The outlaw pitched from his saddle, blood spouting from the .45 caliber hole in his throat.

Another bandido pointed his weapon at Tanaka Tom. He forgot about the marksmen hidden at the windows, but the snipers were not so neglectful. Four rifle slugs tore the outlaw from the back of his horse and slammed his bullet-riddled corpse to the ground. A bandit dragged his sidearm from its holster. Tom's Colt blasted a round through the man's chest before he slid the pistol into leather and closed in on the remaining gang members.

One bandit tried desperately to jack a fresh shell into the chamber of his Winchester when Tom rode up beside him. The *katana* hissed from its scabbard and swung upward in a fast diagonal stroke that sliced his opponent from ribcage to breastbone. The outlaw screamed and fell from his mount. The horse bolted, dragging its dead rider by a booted foot lodged in a stirrup.

The fifth bandit didn't waste time fumbling with the action of his rifle. He braced the gun against his hip and charged the samurai, using his bayonet like a jousting knight. Tom met the attack, both hands fisted around the handle of his sword, his legs hugging the Morgan firmly to retain his balance in the saddle.

The bayonet thrust out viciously. The samurai weaved out of reach as the bandit struggled to keep from being pitched from his horse by his own momentum. Tom's *katana* slashed with the speed of a striking cobra. The outlaw bellowed in agony before he dived to the ground and died. A long scarlet gash between his shoulder blades revealed Tanaka Tom had severed his spine.

Fidel Alverez and eight of his men charged down the center of the street, weapons blazing. Oscar Brill poked the twin barrels of his shotgun through the window of his undertaker's shop and squeezed the trigger. A burst of buckshot peppered the side of El Halcón's black stallion. The animal collapsed, hurtling its rider to the ground hard.

"Got you, you sonofabitch!" the mortician exclaimed.

Two mounted bandidos fired five pistol rounds into the undertaker's window. Three found flesh. Oscar Brill fell heavily to the floor, his shirt soaked by blood.

"Wonder . . ." he rasped, blood rising into his mouth. "Wonder what kinda funeral I'll get. Sure hope the town don't give me a cut-rate one. No, sir." Brill chuckled despite the terrible pain in his chest. "Just when business was about to . . ." Then he was dead and no longer concerned with earthly matters.

Clem Porter's Greener belched a deadly cluster of

buckshot that nearly chopped one of Brill's killers in half. The former town drunk retreated back into the general store before the other bandido could fire at the new threat. Matt Wilkins's shotgun roared from the barber shop and transformed the gunman's chest into gory pulp and threw him from the saddle.

Three bandits dismounted and hurried along the plankwalk to the sheriff's office. Convinced that the primary reason for the raid was to free Carlos, the ambitious trio planned to accomplish this feat and win recognition and some sort of financial reward from their leader. Two bandits positioned themselves on both sides of the door and the third raised a booted foot and smashed the lock with a solid kick.

The door swung open and a .12 gauge shotgun blast sent the exposed outlaw sprawling into the street, his body reduced to butchered meat clad in tattered rags. Before the remaining pair could respond to the loss of their comrade, Tanaka Tom silently emerged from the alley.

One of the bandidos screeched and dropped his pistol. His fellow outlaw stared in horror as a long red-dyed blade burst from the man's chest. A remarkable figure, dressed in a strange costume, thrust a Colt into the startled bandit's face and squeezed the trigger.

The samurai placed a foot on his first victim and pulled the blade of his *katana* from the back of the corpse. Sheriff Newton emerged from the office, the smoking Greener in his hands.

"How are we doin', Tom?" the lawman asked.

"We are busy," the samurai replied simply, speaking with remarkable clarity through his mask.

As if to confirm Tanaka Tom's statement, two mounted bandits galloped toward them, firing pistols at the pair. The samurai's Colt snarled, tearing a hole in the closest rider's chest and dropping him to the ground. To Newton's amazement, Tom holstered his revolver and leaped into the street to meet the other charging horseman.

The rider tried to redirect the aim of his gun at the macabre figure standing before his galloping mount. Tom raised the *katana* in a two-handed grip, overhead and advanced quickly. The bandido grinned. The loco hombre in the devil clothing planned to slash him from the saddle as he rode by. The bastardo would get the biggest and final surprise of his life, for the outlaw intended to trample the samurai under his stallion's hooves!

However, Tanaka Tom wasn't playing by anyone's rules but his own. His sword chopped down hard, his legs wide and the knees bent to allow his entire body to execute the treacherous stroke. The horse whinnied pitifully and tumbled headlong into the street. The samurai had cut off the animal's right foreleg. It somersaulted awkwardly, crushing the hapless rider who had been too startled to abandon his saddle. Tom stepped forward and ended the beast's suffering with another *katana* slash.

Two more mounted outlaws replaced their slain comrades. Hal Newton's scatter-gun boomed its second barrel of buckshot. One rider's chest and face vanished among strawberry pellet wounds before he fell from the saddle.

The samurai deftly sidestepped the other bandido's charging steed and swung his bloodied sword in a powerful stroke too fast for any watching eye to follow. The horse's head seemed to pop from its body and fell to the street like a ghastly knight for a Titan's chessboard. The animal followed, crumbling onto its side, blood gushing from the stump of its neck.

The horrified bandit managed to pull his leg from the dead beast and rose unsteadily to his feet, his eyes locked on the decapitated mount with disbelief. Tanaka Tom swiftly closed in on the outlaw. The man reacted

194

too slowly to the samurai's advance. Before he could aim his revolver at Tom, the slanted point of the sword plunged into the hollow of his throat. The Six-gun Samurai pulled the blade from the dying man and kicked the gun out of his hand in case he survived long enough to pull the trigger.

He examined the street and discovered no more opponents, but continuous gunshots from the surrounding buildings told him the battle was not yet won. He marched to the plankwalk and moved to an alley between the saloon and general store.

"Jesus," Clem Porter whispered, staring out the window of the general store. "It looks like a slaughter house out there!" He licked his lips, wishing he could have just one drink to settle his nerves, yet he realized he could never touch alcohol again, because he could never stop at *one* drink. "I almost feel sorry for them fellers!"

The samurai stopped as he heard voices within the alley.

"For crissake, one of you gimme some ammunition!" Lonny Philips urged desperately.

"My own weapon is empty," Lazaro Morales snapped. "Get some cartridges from Raul. The fat fool managed to lose *both* his rifle and pistol!"

"My horse was shot out from under me," Rodriguez whined. "Is that my fault? I was lucky to escape with my life!"

"Yore luck is gonna run out if'n you don't gimme that ammo belt right now!" the black bandido growled.

All three men fell silent when the incredible figure of the Six-gun Samurai, in full armor, appeared in the mouth of the alley. Lazaro dropped the shell he'd been about to feed into his rifle's magazine. Lonny reversed his grip on the empty Henry carbine and seized it by the barrel like a club. Raul Rodriguez trembled in sheer terror.

"It's him!" the fat man exclaimed. "He wears the mask of death and the uniform of *El Diablo!*"

Lazaro noticed Tom's revolver was in its holster. The samurai advanced slowly, holding his sword ready. "You killed my brother, gringo," Morales hissed. "Now it is your turn to die!"

"Yours or mine," Tom replied calmly. "Come, let us find the answer."

"Lordy, he's crazy as a kitten full o' catnip," Lonny muttered.

Raul recovered from his fear enough to draw the *tanto* knife from his belt.

"Try to smash his skull," Lazaro whispered to Lonny. "He'll block your gun with his sword if you miss and Raul and I will take care of him. He can't get us all."

"I jes' hope he don't get me!" the black man rasped.

The four figures in the alley slowly moved into position, preparing for the deadly contest that would result in sudden, violent death. Tom's sword remained poised, the butt of the handle held near his lower abdomen, its blade extended and the point at eye level.

His eyes shifted in their sockets, watching his opponents. Lonny still gripped his Henry like a club as he cautiously moved forward. Lazaro braced himself and aimed the bayonet on the end of his weapon's barrel at Tom. He stepped behind the black outlaw to Lonny's right. Raul shifted his bulky frame along the wall of the saloon, terrified of the samurai, but hoping to attack him in the safest manner possible—by stabbing him in the back.

Even the gunshots surrounding the combatants seemed subdued by the tension and concentration of their personal confrontation. The battle within Marzo Viento no longer mattered, the rest of the world consisted of illusions and half-forgotten dreams. For those few seconds, nothing was real except the lethal challenge before them. Then Lonny shouted with rage and swung the carbine overhead, aiming the walnut stock at Tom's helmeted head. Lazaro lunged and Raul closed in from behind.

The samurai executed three fast techniques, his movements as fluid as water and more deadly than a tidal wave.

He stepped to Lonny's right, feet splayed at shoulder width and knees bent to lower his body and retain balance. The handle of the *katana* rose above his face mask, braced firmly at the crown of his helmet, the blade forming a razor-sharp bar in the path of Lonny's descending arms. The black bandit couldn't stop the downward swing of his attack in time. Flesh, muscle, and bone struck unyielding metal. Lonny's Henry carbine fell to the ground—dark ebony hands with most of their forearms, still fisted around the barrel.

Lonny screamed and staggered backward, his eyes wide with horror and disbelief as twin rivers of scarlet blood pumped from the stumps of his arms. The pain and shock were too much for him. Lonny Philips wilted to the ground and finished bleeding to death.

Tanaka Tom rose from his squatted stance and turned to meet Lazaro's lunge, the sword handle still braced over his head, revolving until the butt aimed toward the bayonet-thrusting Mexican. The samurai sidestepped the blade at the end of Lazaro's rifle and brought the *katana* down in a powerful stroke. The keen edge struck the bandido between shoulder and neck, slicing through his collarbone and carving his chest open to the solar plexus. His heart and lungs slashed to pieces, Lazaro Morales opened his mouth to scream, but blood bubbled up into his throat and dribbled from his lips. Then he collapsed and died.

Raul Rodriguez had been startled by the samurai's uncanny speed. One moment the man had been standing still and the next he'd moved six feet forward and

197

both Lonny and Lazaro had been cut down. Still, the fat bandido charged Tom's back, hoping the slender blade of the *tanto* knife would penetrate his opponent's armor.

No sooner had the blade of his *katana* dispatched Lazaro Morales, than Tom moved his right arm across his own abdomen, his left hand quickly assuming an overhand grip on the handle of the sword. The blade extended behind the samurai's left hip.

Raul's lunge carried him directly into the merciless steel. The slanted point punctured his fat belly, lancing his stomach and sliding through the layers of fatty tissue to punch through a kidney. The bandido cried out and crumbled to the ground.

Tanaka Tom placed a foot on the dead man's wrist and ground it into the tendons, forcing the hand to open. He bent and relieved the corpse of the *tanto* knife. Then he slid the small scabbard for the weapon from Raul's bloodstained belt. He inserted the blade into its place with a short bow of gratitude to the gods for returning the last of his samurai equipment to him. Then he put the *tanto* into his *obi*.

"Tom, look out!" Amanda Sommer's voice shouted from an upstairs window of the saloon overlooking the alley.

The samurai glanced up to see a masculine fist, filled with a Colt revolver, poke from the window. He dashed from the alley and the pistol boomed, firing a harmless round into the dirt near the retreating man's feet.

Tom darted around the corner, snapped his arm down sharply to shake blood from the blade of his *katana*, and then slid the sword into its scabbard. He jogged into the street, faced the saloon and dove into its newly repaired window, covering his eyes with a forearm. Glass and framework exploded, and the samurai dropped to the sawdust-covered floor on one knee.

A pistol barked, the bullet nicking Tom's *kabuto* helmet. He quickly located two bandidos, one standing behind the bar and the other stationed by the stairs. He drew his Colt and snapped a shot at the man by the counter. The gunman fell back into the bottles and glasses mounted behind the bar and sunk from view.

Tom swung his pistol at the other bandit and squeezed the trigger. The hammer struck an empty chamber. The outlaw smiled coldly and fired his Remington .44 at the samurai. Tanaka Tom propelled himself across the floor, colliding with the legs of a table and chairs. Before the gunman could redirect his aim, Tom turned over the table and moved behind its wide top. He realized the thin wooden shield wouldn't stop a 200 grain bullet, but it would conceal him and make a more difficult target for the bandit.

The Remington snarled, its projectile biting through the table near the samurai's left arm. Tom suddenly rose from the flimsy shelter and hurled two *shurikens* at the startled gunman. The bandido screamed and dropped his revolver. One star-shaped weapon had stabbed deeply into his right biceps and the other had struck high in his chest. The wounded man toppled down the stairs in a moaning heap.

Tom moved across the room toward the stairs when another gunshot arrested his attention. Rafael Montoya, in the upstairs corridor by the railing overlooking the saloon, struggled with Amanda Sommer for posession of the Colt revolver in his fist. His other hand smashed the woman in the face and knocked her to the floor. He swung his pistol at the samurai and thumbed back the hammer.

Tanaka Tom dashed to the bar and vaulted over it nimbly. Although his ears rung from the constant gunshots within the saloon, he still heard the heavy footsteps of the man above him.

Something moved beside Tom. He turned to see the stunned, but murderous, face of the man he'd shot. The bandido rose from the floor, bracing his gun in both hands. Pink fluid mingled with red stains on his shirt where the samurai's bullet had punctured a lung. Blood oozed from the man's tense lips, but his eyes were filled with determination and hate. He knew he was about to die and he wanted to take his killer with him to Hell.

Tom's left hand slapped the barrel of the bandit's pistol downward and his right dipped toward his *obi*. The gun discharged, blasting a bullet into the floor boards by the samurai's feet. The *ho-tachi* short sword whispered from its scabbard and slashed a rapid cross-body stroke. Blood poured from the bandido's slit throat. He dropped his weapon and clamped both hands to the terrible wound as if somehow he could hold back the crimson tide. He failed and dropped to the floor—dead.

A revolver boomed and a bullet chewed off a corner of the bar in front of Tom. Rafael, in the upstairs hall, stood directly above the samurai and now leaned over the railing to fire blindly at his adversary, hoping to get a lucky shot. The second round shattered a whisky bottle behind Tom. He heard the bandit curse in frustration and cock the hammer once more.

Quickly, the samurai unwound the *kusarigama* from around his waist. The seven-foot chain, with its crescent-shaped knife attached to one end and the iron ball at the other, served as an unusual and flexible weapon for Tanaka Tom. The gunman fired another bullet into the wall behind his intended victim. Tom gripped the chain near the ball with his right hand and hopped up onto the counter. He whirled the sickle in his left hand before hurling it upward, pitching the blade in a wide curve overhead.

The crescent knife slammed into the bandido's chest.

He gasped in agony and the Colt fell from limp fingers. Rafael tried to pull the weapon from his bleeding flesh, surprised to feel iron chain links instead of a knife handle. *How'd he do it?* Montoya took his last thoughts with him into eternity. Tom tugged the chain hard and pulled the bandido over the railing like a giant fish attached to a monstrous line. The corpse crashed to the saloon floor ten feet below and twitched twice before lying still.

A bloodthirsty war cry drew Tom's head to the right. The man he'd wounded with the *shurikens* had managed to find enough strength and will power to launch another attack. Holding a bone-handled knife in an overhand grip, the bandit charged Tom with a fury born of anger and pain. The tines of the star-shaped blades jutted from his chest and upper arm like metallic tumors.

Tom gripped the chain of the *kusarigama* near its middle and slashed his arm sideways. The iron ball whirled in a fast, vicious arch before striking the side of the outlaw's head. Skull fragments burst into the bandit's brain like chips of sharpened flint. His eyes rolled upward and he staggered along the length of the bar before sliding to the floor in a lifeless lump.

The batwings swung open and Juan Ruiz entered the saloon. He immediately spied the samurai. Tom released the *kusarigama* and jumped down behind the bar as the bandit fired his rifle from the hip. The slug smashed into the remnants of the mirror behind him. The samurai reached for a *shuriken* in his sash, but he stopped when he heard Juan fumbling with the lever of his weapon. The rifle had jammed.

Tanaka Tom rose and faced El Halcón's second in command. Juan's expression revealed cold determination as he gripped the rifle firmly and aimed the bayonet attached to the muzzle at the samurai. Tom

201

stepped from behind the bar and calmly drew the *katana* from its scabbard. He advanced slowly, watching his opponent, prepared for Juan's lunge. The bandido moved closer, holding his rifle low.

Juan realized he faced an extraordinary foe, but he also knew his own ability with a bayonet was exceptional. He had excelled above all his fellow bandits in the use of cold steel fixed to the end of a long gun. He decided to feint a stab to the gut, then quickly drive the bayonet upward and slam it under the samurai's mask, into his throat.

He thrust his weapon at Tom, prepared to carry out his plan, but the Six-gun Samurai's defense ruined all possibility of its success. Tom side-stepped and moved to his opponent's left in a quick stride. The bayonet thrust into midair and the *katana* rose over Tom's head. The blade swung and struck the side of Juan Ruiz's neck. It cleaved through flesh, muscle, and vertebra like a stalk of bamboo. Juan's head hopped from his body and rolled across the saloon floor, staining the sawdust with yet more blood. A scarlet volcano erupted from the stump of the bandido's neck.

The decapitated body charged across the room, its nervous system still committed to the attack and unaware its host had already died. The bayonet slammed into the bar deeply, bringing the running corpse to a sudden halt. Juan Ruiz collapsed on his rifle, breaking the blade of the bayonet off in the thick wood. The gruesome corpse shuddered briefly and finally accepted oblivion.

"Tom?" Amanda Sommer's voice called from upstairs. "Tom, are you all right?"

"Yes," he nodded curtly, his ears straining to listen to the sounds outside.

The shooting had stopped.

The Six-gun Samurai peered cautiously over the batwings. Corpses, horses as well as human, littered the

202

street. Townsfolk slowly emerged from the buildings, weapons still in their sweaty hands. A wounded man moaned and a woman wept, but the sounds of battle had ceased. Tom stepped onto the plankwalk and nodded with grim satisfaction.

Marzo Viento had won.

Nineteen

Hal Newton wearily slung his Greener shotgun over his shoulder and crossed the street to join Tanaka Tom. "We whupped 'em," the sheriff sighed. "Reckon your karma was workin' for you like you figured."

"One does not try to predetermine Destiny," the samurai corrected. "One merely accepts it."

Clem Porter jogged up to the lawmen. "Matt Wilkins and a few of his boys are holdin' three of the bandits prisoner over by the stable," he announced. "All the rest are dead."

"How'd our side do?" Newton inquired.

"Well, I reckon it could'a been a whole lot worse," Clem replied. "Oscar Brill is dead, so is Joel Stewart and Mabel is takin' it mighty hard. Two of Wilkins's boys are on their way to the happy huntin' ground too. That feller with his jaw wired together got winged, but it ain't serious. Jacob Fritter got it a lot worse. Damn near tore his arm off. I won't be surprised if it has to be amputated."

"Not good," Newton remarked. "But like you say, it could'a been a whole lot worse."

"You can add Bart to the list, Hal," Amanda Sommer told him as she appeared from the swinging doors. "One of those bandits chased him into the storage room and blew his brains out."

"I'm sorry, Amanda," Newton said.

"Me too," she sighed. "Reckon now I'll have to serve the drinks personal. Too bad about that damn window gettin' busted again," she smiled at Tom. "But under the circumstances, I don't really mind at all."

"Well, Deputy," the sheriff mused. "You wanna come along and help me put our new prisoners under arrest? Sort'a be your last official act before you turn in your badge."

"I'd be honored, Hal," Tom replied, surprised by the twinge of regret he experienced with the knowledge he'd soon be leaving Marzo Viento. He had grown to like and admire Hal Newton. The trail would seem strangely lonely when he returned to his quest for vengeance.

The samurai and Sheriff Newton walked together toward the livery stable. "Gonna be sorry to see you leave, Tom," the senior lawman remarked. "You're one hell of a man."

"So are you," Tanaka Tom said sincerely. "I am glad we . . ."

His sentence stopped sharply when he saw a tall, black clad figure suddenly rise from the street. El Halcón whirled the *bolas* overhead twice and hurled it at the pair. The weapon sizzled toward Hal Newton's head like a flying buzzsaw.

The samurai leaped forward, drawing his *katana*. The long ribbon of steel seemed to appear in his hand by magic. The sword flashed in the sunlight and met the whistling *bolas*. Three lead-filled balls hurled in different directions and fell harmlessly. The rawhide cords dropped to Tom's feet like twisted, dead serpents.

"Don't make another move, Alverez!" Newton warned, aiming his shotgun at the bandido leader.

205

El Halcón spat angrily. "Shoot if you wish," he declared. "I have no deisre to face the indignity of a hanging."

"Thanks for savin' my life, Tom," the sheriff said, his eyes and the muzzles of his Greener, still trained on Alverez.

. "It was my debt, Hal. My obligation is complete," the samurai replied. "But I would have done so anyway," he added in a soft voice.

"I believe you," Newton commented, feeling a warm kinship as well as gratitude toward Tom.

"Since I am to die for my so-called crimes, may I have a last request?" El Halcón asked, folding his arms akimbo on his chest.

"Don't expect us to grant it, feller," the sheriff growled.

"It isn't your decision to make," Alverez stated. "Is it, *Señor* Fletcher?"

"What's he talkin' about, Tom?" Newton inquired.

"We were to have a duel today," the bandit chief declared. "Remember, Fletcher? You challenged me, no?"

"I remember," the samurai replied.

"Forget it, Alverez," the sheriff snapped. "Tom don't have to . . ."

"You will have your duel," Tanaka Tom told the bandit.

"Tom!" the sheriff exclaimed. "That's crazy! You don't have to prove nothin' to this bastard."

"He is correct," the samurai insisted. "I challenged him to a duel and he accepted. He has a right to face me on the field of honor and I am obliged to agree to his terms."

"Sí," El Halcón smiled coldly. "And *I* have choice of weapons."

"This is crazy!" Newton muttered.

"Let's see," Alverez mused. "I don't imagine the

townsfolk or the sheriff here would be willing to let me have a gun, even one with only a single bullet. I'm not foolish enough to choose swords and you've ruined my *bolas*. What shall we use?"

"The choice is yours," the samurai stated simply.

El Halcón smiled with evil delight. "Machetes!"

The sun sunk below the horizon and sent streaks of orange through the sky. Some of the light beams appeared blood red before the great orb of daylight vanished, an uncanny introduction to the event about to take place in the streets of Marzo Viento.

Torches were lit to ward off the darkness. The citizens of the town stood along the plankwalk and watched while the two most deadly men that had ever set foot in their community, met for a final battle to the death.

El Halcón stood silently, his face proud and arrogant in spite of the fact he knew there would be no escape for him. Whether he died in the duel or at the end of a rope, he realized it was finished. The Alverez heritage had been destroyed forever. His life no longer mattered, nor the life of his brother. He had refused to see Carlos. Why further his feeling of defeat and bitterness by looking upon his worthless sibling who had never lived as a proper Alverez and would certainly die as a coward?

Fidel Alverez had but one comforting thought, but it proved strong enough to allow him to stand tall, with his head held high like the bird of prey of his nickname's origin. He would kill Fletcher. More than anyone else, the samurai had been responsible for his losses. After he'd slain his archenemy, perhaps he'd turn on the crowd, swinging his machete like a madman and forcing them to kill him. It would be a better end than hanging—a better death than the one he would deal to Tanaka Tom Fletcher.

The Six-gun Samurai had removed his armor since El Halcón had complained that it would be an unfair advantage in the duel. Clad in his customary short kimono jacket, Levis trousers and *obi*, Tanaka Tom carried no weapon when he stepped into the street to face his opponent.

"Are you ready, Tom?" Sheriff Newton asked. No one inquired if the bandido was prepared.

"Give us the knives, please," the samurai replied simply.

Hal Newton solemnly handed him a machete taken from one of the dead bandits. Tom's expression did not betray his displeasure while he tested the weapon in his skilled hands. The jungle knife was nearly as long as a *ho-tachi*, but heavier and more unwieldly to the *kenjutsu*-trained samurai. The wooden handle felt crude and alien in his grasp. Tom swung the machete in several practice strokes, both one-handed and two-handed grips, to familiarize himself with it.

Since no one wanted to get close to El Halcón, let alone be responsible for putting a weapon in his hands, the citizens of Marzo Viento were surprised when Clem Porter volunteered for the unpopular task. The former town drunk walked six feet in front of the bandit chief and bent to thrust the point of the machete into the ground.

"Sorry there wasn't time for me to dull the blade up a bit," Clem told Alverez.

El Halcón stepped forward and bent to retrieve the knife. Clem drew back his head, worked saliva into his mouth and spat into the outlaw's face. Alverez seized the machete and angrily jerked it from the earth. He turned sharply, but Clem had already retreated to the plankwalk. The bandit wiped the spit from his fierce face and swung around to face Tanaka Tom.

"I am ready, *Señor* Fletcher," he declared.

Tom nodded and stepped forward.

The combatants advanced slowly. Tension filled the atmosphere like electrified air. Flickering yellow light from the torches danced across the duelists' hard, determined faces. Their dark eyes blazed with expectation as they drew closer. The crowd held its collective breath and waited, their spines tingling with excitement and apprehension.

El Halcón launched the first attack. He feinted a downward chop at Tom's head, then swiftly altered the swing to a diagonal slash to his opponent's neck. The samurai blocked Alverez's machete with the flat of his blade and executed a sweeping stroke at the bandit's midsection. El Halcón nimbly jumped back, but the keen edge of Tom's jungle knife sliced through cloth and broke the surface of Alverez's skin.

The bandit leader ignored the shallow cut to his belly and thrust his weapon at Tom's chest. The samurai's blade parried the attack, but El Halcón moved with the change in the knife's direction, twisting his wrist sharply to slash the machete into his adversary's rib cage. Tanaka Tom weaved quickly and felt the sting of sharp metal bite his flesh. Blood oozed onto the side of his kimono as the two men squared off once more.

"A cut here and a cut there, Fletcher," El Halcón hissed. "That's how you will die!"

He swung his machete like a cutlass. Steel clanged when the two blades met. Before Tom could follow with a counterattack, Alverez's leg lashed out at the samurai's thigh. The bandit's spur ripped open Tom's leg above the knee. The samurai's swing missed its mark and El Halcón's blade slammed the weapon aside. His arm streaked forward, his fist clenched around the machete handle, struck Tom's jaw hard and knocked him to the ground.

Tanaka Tom fell on his back with a muffled grunt.

Alverez's boot stomped onto his opponent's wrist, pinning the samurai's hand and knife to the ground. El Halcón raised his machete overhead in a two-hand grip.

"Too easy, Fletcher," he scoffed. Then he swung the heavy blade at Tom's face.

The samurai jerked his head aside and the machete struck the earth less than an inch from his ear. Tom's leg rose quickly and drove a solid ball-of-the-foot kick to Alverez's kidney. The bandit groaned painfully. The samurai arched his back and threw both feet into a powerful kick that caught his opponent in the small of the back and pitched him headlong to the ground.

Tanaka Tom scrambled to his feet rapidly, but El Halcón rolled with his fall and rose just as fast. The bandit swung a false stroke at Tom's chest. The samurai's blade slapped the attacking knife. Suddenly, El Halcón launched a high kick. The spur slashed Tom's forearm and his fingers popped open, dropping the machete.

Alverez chuckled with arrogant confidence and closed in on his unarmed opponent. Tom assumed a karate T-*dachi* stance, his hands poised at chest and hip level for defensive action. El Halcón dropped to one knee and slashed his jungle knife at the samurai's lead leg, attempting to cripple his opponent.

Tom bent his knee and raised his leg high above the sweeping steel. The blade whistled harmlessly through air. The samurai straighted his leg and slammed his boot full into Alverez's face. Blood squirted from the bandido's shattered nose. He fell, rolled sideways and jumped upright before Tom could retrieve his weapon.

El Halcón faked a thrust to Tom's face, then executed a fast sideways slash at the samurai. Tanaka Tom's hands chopped into the aggressor's forearm like twin axes. The double-*shuto* stroke blocked the attack and jarred the machete from El·Halcón's grasp. The big knife fell to the ground and Tom swiftly snapped a *ura ken* backfist blow to Alverez's mouth.

The bandido staggered, but didn't fall. He charged the samurai like a fighting cock, leaping into the air to thrust a booted foot at Tom's face, trying to gouge out an eye with his deadly spur.

Tanaka Tom side-stepped the attack and moved behind Alverez while his opponent was still in midair. His hard forearm slammed a powerful *kote* blow to El Halcón's lower back. The outlaw was knocked off balance and fell heavily to the ground.

The Six-gun Samurai dove forward in a quick shoulder-roll and landed beside his discarded machete, grabbing the handle and rising to his feet with the jungle knife in his fist. El Halcón rose slowly, staring at his now-armed adversary.

"Pick up your weapon," Tom ordered coldly.

Alverez gathered up his machete and drew closer.

The blades clashed when both men attacked simultaneously. El Halcón's free hand seized the samurai's wrist behind his machete and twisted the heavy blade away from his face to slash his own weapon at the side of Tom's neck. The samurai's strong fingers caught his opponent's sleeve, jerking the attacking arm aside.

Their faces nearly touching, the combatants struggled to break free and deliver a fatal blow. Alverez raked a spur into Tom's calf muscle, forcing a snarl of pain from the samurai. Suddenly, Tanaka Tom folded both knees and sat down, pulling the bandit forward. He landed on his back and raised a foot to El Halcón's midsection. Tom straightened his leg and hurled the startled Alverez overhead in a swift *tomoe-nage* throw.

El Halcón crashed to the ground in a stunned heap. Tanaka Tom's body seemed to leap up to a standing position without moving his limbs. He whirled to face his opponent. Alverez rose unsteadily to his feet and advanced.

211

The bandit chief swung his blade at Tom's wrist, trying to disarm and maim his enemy with a single blow. The samurai jerked his arm out of range and slashed El Halcón across the chest rapidly. Alverez staggered backward, blood oozing from the deep gash in his pectoral muscles. Yet, he bellowed with rage and whirled his weapon in a high overhead attack.

Tanaka Tom's machete rose, the blade meeting the descending knife. A shred of a second seemed to extend into eternity as the two men's arms remained raised, their weapons locked together, and the aura of death filled the air.

The samurai brought his machete down with all his force. The edge struck the top of El Halcón's skull with a stomach-turning crunch. Hair, skin and bone were cleaved through in a single blow. Fidel Alverez released his jungle knife and screamed. He stumbled away from Tom, the machete still firmly lodged in his head. Pink and gray brains dribbled from the ghastly wound, accompanied by a stream of crimson that poured between the unseeing eyes.

El Halcón woodenly raised his hands to the handle of the weapon jammed into his skull, but the last flickering of life departed before he could yank the machete free. The once feared El Halcón collapsed into the dust and died.

EPILOGUE

The Six-gun Samurai spread a sheet of parchment on the table in his room and carefully dipped the stiff horse hair tip of his whale bone writing brush into the ornate ink well. Slowly, he stroked the pen across the paper and formed the delicate ideographs of *Kan-ji*, the written language of Japanese.

Most Honored Father,

The man I sought in the territory called New Mexico died before I could question him or personally dispatch his spirit from his body. Yet, although I did not accomplish my original task, my heart is not heavy with disappointment. I have learned much these past three days—much about the country of the United States of America and its people. It is strange to return to the land of my birth and discover so many things that I did not appreciate as a child.

In numerous ways, the Americans are not unlike we Japanese. In other ways, they differ, but in a manner that is neither uncivilized or disagreeable. Although they share neither our culture nor our beliefs, I have found many to be men of honor and courage. I fought beside men willing to die for what they believed in. I saw a man broken by excess of

213

alcohol become a brave warrior when circumstances forced him to act on behalf of others instead of himself. I've witnessed great acts of loyalty and devotion to principles that would do justice to a samurai.

You once told me, Father, that a wise man never ceases to learn. My wisdom has thus increased. I have learned that honor and courage are not restricted to nationality and culture. They are qualities inherent in men of all lands. Although they do not call their particular code *bushido*, they believe in it and live their lives accordingly—with courage and honor.

I also have learned greater faith in the ways of karma, for although I did not find the man called Eddie Mears in time to question him, my destiny steered me to the town of Marzo Viento where I learned of another member of my archenemy's forces who promises to be a far greater prize than the one I lost. Today, while reading a newspaper to improve my understanding of English—both written and spoken—I acquired new information about a man named Carlton Gray who served with Colonel Hollister in the 251st Ohio Regiment.

Gray has been apprehended for illegally prospecting for gold in the Black Hills of a territory known as the Dakotas. In the past, I have encountered Hollister's schemes to acquire such precious metals as gold and silver. This may be another of his sinister plots. I must find this man Gray and learn what he knows about Hollister's whereabouts. As I have stated before, America is far larger than we had suspected. My journey to the Dakotas will be long and I must begin immediately.

May your karma be fruitful, Honored Father, and may the gods and our respected ancestors, look upon you with favor.

Tanaka Tom Fletcher stamped the letter with the traditional seal of the Tanaka Family—his family as surely as the blood kin he had sworn to avenge. Thoughtfully, he placed his writing brush aside.

GLOSSARY

JAPANESE

Bajutsu—Samurai horsemanship.

Bojutsu—Stick fighting martial art using a long stave.

Bushido—The code of honor and conduct of the samurai.

Cha—Green tea.

Chunin—Subleaders of a *ninja* clan.

Dachi—A karate fighting stance.

Dai Nippon—Japan.

Ebira—Archer's quiver.

Fumikomi—Karate stamp kick.

Gedan uchi—A leg sweep with a *bojutsu* stave.

Genin—A *ninja* espionage agent.

Gyaku-yoko-uchi—Butt stroke with a bojutsu stave.

Ho-tachi—Samurai short sword.

Ippon-seoi-nage—Shoulder throw.

Jonin—Chief or leader of a *ninja* clan.

Jutte—An iron trunchen used by samurai policemen.

Kabuto—Samurai helmet.

Kai—A boat oar used as a weapon by Okinawan martial artists.

Kan-ji—Japanese written language.

Karma—One's individual destiny according to Zen.

Katana—Samurai long sword.

Ki—Inner strength, unites mind, body, and spirit.

Kote—Karate forearm stroke.

215

Kusarigama—Chain weapon with an iron ball attached to one end and a sickle at the other.

Kyoketsu-shogi—A double-bladed knife attached to a long cord, employed in a manner similar to a *Kusarigama*.

Kyujutsu—Samurai combat archery.

Maedate—Hornlike ornament on a samurai helmet.

Mae-geri-kekomi—Karate front kick.

Mae-geri-keage—Front snap kick.

Maru-bo—A stave used in *bojutsu*.

Mawashi-geri—Karate roundhouse kick.

Naginata—Japanese halbred.

Ninja—A secret society of espionage agents and assassins.

Sake—Rice wine.

Seiken—Karate "forefist" punch, using first two big knuckles.

Seppuku—Ritual of suicide by disembowelment to compensate for dishonor. Often incorrectly called *hara-kiri*.

Shikoru—Neck protector on samurai helmet.

Shuko—"Tiger claws," metal claws used by *ninja* for scaling walls and as close combat weapons.

Shuriken—A spike- or star-shaped weapon thrown at an opponent. The use of these devices is called *shuri-kenjutsu*.

Shuto—A karate chop with the side of the hand.

Tanto—Samurai knife.

Tomoe-nage—"Circle" throw.

Tsuki-komi—Thrust stroke with a *bojutsu* stave.

Tsuru-banshiri—Breastplate of a samurai's wooden armor.

Ura-ken—Karate back-fist blow.

Ushiro-keage-geri—Karate rear heel kick.

Zazen—Breathing technique of Japanese martial arts.

SPANISH

Aldea—A small village.

Aldehvela—Little village, hamlet.

¡Ayudannos!—Help us!

Bandido—Bandit.

Bolas—A South American weapon made of three cords with lead-filled balls, thrown at a target.

Brujo—A "male witch," a wizard.

Buenas días—"Good day."

Cabrón—Insult—suggesting the man has an unfaithful wife.

Cachorro—Rude, ill-bred person.

¡Callete!—Quiet!

Capitán—Captain.

Casa—House.

Cuchillo—Knife.

Diablo—Devil.

El—The.

Espada—Sword.

Estancia—Estate.

Federales—Mexican troops serving as federal police.

Gracias—Thank you.

Halcón—Hawk.

Hombre—Man.

Indio—Indian.

Machismo—Manliness.

¡Maldecir mi hermano!—Curse my brother! or To hell with my brother!

Mayor—Major.

Muerte—Dead.

Patrón—Boss, landord.

Por favor—"For a favor." Please.

¡Que la chigada!—"Oh, fuck!"

Señor—"Sir" or "Mister."

Sí—Yes.

Tigre—Tiger. In South America, this generally refers to a jaguar, not an actual tiger.

Vaya con Dios—"Go with God." Good-bye.